Triangles

6

NIA RICH

Also by Nia Rich

Never Going Back

My Love Is Deeper

F--k Boy

Seduced by a Savage

Triangles 1-5

Triangles 6

Written by: Nia Rich
Copyright © 2018 Nia Rich

All rights reserved.

Cover: Tina Shivers
Editor: Venitia Crawford-Fergus

This is a work of fiction. Names, characters, places are either the product of the authors imagination or are used fictitiously and any resemblance to actual persons, living or dead, business establishments, events, or locals, is entirely coincidental.

Previously in Triangles…

Aleyah

Aleyah and Shalita followed security as they escorted Karina outside of the nightclub on New Year's Eve. She was still yelling and fussing about Eazy's date. Once they were outside, Aleyah and Shalita began trying to calm Karina down.

"Karina, you need to calm down." Shalita said.

"Yes, you do best friend." Aleyah said.

"Nah that dumb bitch needs her ass whooped." Karina said loudly.

"Seriously it is too cold outside for you to be this hot." Shalita said.

"Especially over somebody that you're not with anymore." Aleyah said.

"Honestly, all I wanted to know was why I wasn't on the list for the party. He put everyone else on the list. He even put my best friend on the list, and that bitch that he was with, but not me. The woman that has his child. He is always leaving me out of shit, and then that bitch he was with wanna roll her eyes, so I checked her ass."

"Yea, but you're drunk, and that drama was unnecessary. Did it ever occur to you that he doesn't want you there? That's why he never invites you." Shalita said.

"Yea, and now we are out here in the freezing cold on New Year's Eve, when we could be drinking and partying." Aleyah said.

"Fuck this party and this club. I should go back in there and finish whooping that cheap-ass hoe ass." Karina yelled.

Karina stormed back towards the club's entrance, but Shalita grabbed her and pulled her back. "No, you're not. You're going home." she said.

"Why? Why can't I beat a bitch ass for the New Year?" Karina asked.

"Because you're drunk best friend, and I'm not going to jail tonight messing with you, so you need to go. I need to leave anyways to get home to Lamar, so I'll walk with y'all." Aleyah said.

Shalita wrapped one of her arms around Karina's and turned her around to walk towards the parking ramp. Aleyah walked on the other side of Karina. Karina was still upset and ranting all the way back to her car. Aleyah helped Shalita put Karina into the passenger side of her car. Shalita took the keys and walked over to the driver's side. Aleyah hugged Karina and told her that she would check on her the next day before closing the passenger side door.

"You good?" she asked Shalita.

"Yea. I got her. Thank you." Shalita responded.

"You're welcome. Happy New Year." Aleyah said.

"I know right. You too." Shalita said before getting into the car.

Aleyah chuckled as she headed to her car. She shook her head when she thought about the whole scene at the club. Karina had always been a fire cracker, but she had never seen her act like that. Aleyah took her keys out of her purse, and then turned to wave goodbye to Shalita when she drove past.

Aleyah unlocked her car, opened the door, and before she could get in, someone grabbed her from behind, and put their hand with a rag over her mouth and nose, and pulled one of her arms behind her back. She tried to scream and fight with her lose arm, but the person was strong.

"Shut the fuck up." the person said.

Aleyah immediately recognized the voice. It was Niko. He stood there and held her like that while watching his surroundings to make sure that no one was coming for a while. She struggled, but she couldn't get free. Eventually, she felt herself getting weak, and then everything went black.

After her body went limp, he kept his hand over her face for a few more second to make sure that she was out. He kept his eyes moving back and forth checking his surroundings while he stood there with her. He put the rag into his back pocket, closed her car door, picked Aleyah up, and carried her limp body to his car. He gently sat her in the passenger seat of his car, put a seatbelt on her, and closed the door. He got into the car on the driver's side, took his black hood off his head, pulled out of the parking spot, and drove out of the parking ramp.

Triangles

6

NIA RICH

Prologue

It was New Year's Eve night. Lamar and the guys were standing in the garage talking and smoking. Lamar noticed that Niko's energy was off from the moment he arrived. Niko was standoffish, and he kept giving Lamar funny looks. Lamar figured Niko was just drunk, but Niko kept hitting him with sly comments. Lamar kept laughing Niko's comments off, but Niko wasn't letting up. He was in another mindset, so he kept trying to push Lamar's buttons. He was slowly, but surely ticking Lamar off.

"I don't know what to do about my wife man. Seems like she is always in a mood." one of Lamar's friends said.

"Man, women are always in a mood." Lamar's cousin said.

"Sometimes you just have to give them their space." Lamar said.

Niko laughed and said, "This dude thinks he the shit. You ain't shit bruh."

He passed the blunt to one of Lamar's friends.

Lamar laughed and said, "Yea aight."

"Anyways. When my wife gets in a mood, I just give her some space. Eventually she comes looking for some attention."

"Yea I guess you're right."

Niko laughed and said, "Why y'all listening to this weak ass advise. This dude doesn't know what he is talking about."

Lamar laughed and replied, "Man shut the fuck up. I'm the one who is married; not you, so I know what I am talking about."

Niko said, "You know your wife runs you bruh. She be having this dudes panties in a bunch."

Lamar chuckled and said, "Whatever bruh. Go on with that panties shit bruh, my wife doesn't run shit. I'm the man of my house."

Niko was rubbing Lamar the wrong way, and he knew it. It gave Niko pleasure to see Lamar's anger building, so he kept pushing Lamar's buttons.

"I feel you bruh. I have to remind my girl that all the time. Especially when she gets to yacking at the mouth talking crazy." Lamar's friend said.

He slapped hands with Lamar, hit the blunt, and passed it to Lamar.

"Shit, I shut my girl up with this D." Lamar's cousin said.

"That's another way to do it cuz." Lamar said.

Everyone laughed, and then Niko said, "You tryna be the relationship guru. You need to shut the fuck up."

Lamar looked at Niko and everyone else did the same. They could feel the tension brewing, but no one was saying anything about it. Lamar was starting to wonder what Niko's problem was, and so was everyone else that was standing out there in the garage with them.

"Aight bruh, you on some other shit right now."
Lamar said before hitting the blunt.

*"Nah, I'm on some real shit. You tryna give advice
and your shit ain't right bruh."*

*Lamar laughed, passed the blunt, and said, "You
don't even know what you're talking about bruh."*

*Niko laughed, hit the blunt, and then he said, "But I
do. I bet you don't even know where your wife is right
now."*

*Lamar's energy changed, and then he said, "I
always know where my wife is. She is with her friends at
the club."*

*"No, you don't. That's what you think bruh?"
Lamar asked, and then he started laughing. "Your wife
could be fucking over you right now and you wouldn't even
know.*

*He passed the blunt to Lamar's cousin. Niko had
finally pushed Lamar to the point of snapping. He was tired
of Niko's sly remarks and comments. Lamar wanted to
know what Niko's problem was.*

"What is you saying bruh? You got something that you need to get off your chest?" Lamar asked angrily.

The garage fell silent as everyone realized that the conversation had turned serious.

"I'm just saying your bitch ass don't even know who your wife could be fucking around with bruh. Cause you're too lax. You don't know what she's doing when she leaves the crib. You don't even know if your wife could be fucking around with me. I could be fucking your wife right now."

"Ooooh shit." one of Lamar's friends said.

"What? Are you fucking my wife bruh?"

"Bitch I might be. What the fuck you gonna do about it?"

Lamar swung and hit Niko in the jaw. Niko grabbed his jaw and started swinging back. He hit Lamar in the mouth, but Lamar hit him in the gut and knocked him off balance. Everyone else in the garage started to scatter while the two men fought in the garage. Lamar was hitting Niko so fast that he didn't have the time to swing back. All he could do was put Lamar in a choke hold, but Lamar broke out of it and slammed Niko onto the cold concrete.

*"You bitch ass muthafucka! You got me fucked up!"
Lamar yelled.*

*The other guys jumped in it to break them up.
Lamar's cousin pulled Lamar off Niko, and one of the other
guys pulled Niko out of the garage.*

*"Punk ass muthafucka! I can take your wife if I
want to!"*

"Get the fuck from around my house!"

"Bet! I will bruh! I'll be back though!" Niko yelled.

He got into his car and drove off.

*"Damn what was that shit about?" Lamar's cousin
asked as they closed the garage door and walked back into
the house.*

"I don't know, but I need to call my wife."

*Lamar called Aleyah's phone, but it rang through to
voicemail. He called again, but he got the voicemail again,
so Lamar sent Aleyah a text and told her to call him as
soon as possible. That was one of the many times that
Lamar would call Aleyah that night with no answer or
response from her.*

Chapter 1

Aleyah

Aleyah woke up in a fog. She couldn't tell where she was. At first, she felt like she was lying down, but then she realized that she was sitting up. Her eyes felt heavy, so she didn't try to open them right away. The first thing she heard was a radio DJ talking. Her ears tuned into the conversation they were having about some celebrity gossip, and then she heard a car driving over bumps and ridges in the road. She slowly opened her eyes. It took her eyes a while to adjust to the sunlight shining through the window. Judging by the way the sun was set, she could tell that it was early in the morning. Her guess was that it was in between five or six o'clock in the morning. Once her eyes adjusted, she started seeing snow on the ground and trees without leaves going by fast. Aleyah started asking herself why she was seeing naked trees, and then it suddenly hit her. She had been snatched up the night before. The last thing she remembered was a hand around her face and a slightly sweet aroma before she blacked out. Aleyah jerked awake, sat up, and looked at the driver.

Niko smiled at her and said, "Hey beautiful. Good morning."

Aleyah snapped, "Niko what the fuck!? Where am I!? Let me out of this car now!"

"Oooo. Somebody is waking up angry." he chuckled.

"Where are we!? Where are you taking me!?" Aleyah repeated.

"Calm down. You're with me baby. We are somewhere between Iowa and Illinois. I'm taking you home, so we can get married."

"You fucking kidnapped me! Let me out of this car now!"

"I'm not letting you out of anything, so you can just sit back and enjoy the ride."

Aleyah started swinging at him. She punched him a few times, and then she grabbed the steering wheel and jerked it making the car swerve. Niko blocked most of the punches accept one. When he felt the car swerve, he snatched the wheel back straight, and then he smacked Aleyah extremely hard. Aleyah grabbed her face, leaned over, and started crying.

"Now sit back and settle the fuck down!" he yelled. "Fuck is your problem!? See what you made me do!?"

Niko looked at his reflection through the review mirror. There was a little scratch by his eye where she had hit him.

"Look at this shit you did to my fucking eye!"

He grabbed the back of her shirt and pushed her. She stayed leaning over with her face in her hands. She was crying hysterically.

"Shut the fuck up Aleyah! Don't make this harder than it needs to be. Just sit back and chill."

Aleyah lifted up and said, "Just take me home Niko. I have a son!"

"What home? Lamar already knows, and he is done with you. Like I said, you're coming with me. We're going to get married and be together forever."

"Don't you think somebody is going to come searching for me eventually?" she asked wiping tears from her face.

"I'm not worried about all that, so just enjoy the ride. Please don't make me do you like my first wife."

"What first wife?"

"The one that is in the cemetery in Chicago. She was my first love, but she didn't want to act right. I go and visit her from time to time."

"Are you serious?"

"Dead serious. You're about to meet her. I'm going to take you there first before I take you home to my family in Virginia. I need to ask her for her blessings."

"You can't do this!" Aleyah yelled.

"Fuck you mean? Yes, I can and I will."

"Niko, I need to go home to my family!"

"You tryna go home to him, huh?" Niko pulled a gun from his waist and set it on his lap with the barrel facing her. "Is that what you want to do?" he asked.

"Really Niko? You're going to pull a gun on me?"

"Don't make me use it."

Aleyah fell quiet.

"That's what I thought. Now, shut the fuck up and enjoy this ride."

She started searching her pockets for her phone.

"I have your phone. It's dead anyway, so stop. I 've been driving all night, so we'll be at our first stop soon."

Aleyah stopped searching, shook her head, sat back in the seat, and looked out the window.

Chapter 2

Riley

When Mike and Riley arrived at the hospital, the hospital staff put Riley in a room, had her change into a hospital gown, and then they hooked her up to a bunch of monitors. The doctor stopped in to check on her, and then the doctor left. Mike sat by the bed and watched television with Riley for a while. By time the sun came up, people started trickling in. Raelyn was the first to show up with Paris. Riley and Raelyn 's parents showed up next, and then Taji arrived. Cherry was the last one to show up.

It was early morning on New Year's Day and everyone was at the hospital anticipating the arrival of

Riley's first baby. Aleyah and Eazy were the only two missing. Everyone was sitting around Riley's room talking to her and keeping her company. Riley's dad had just cracked a joke about how big Riley's belly was when the hospital door swung open and Jamir walked in. Jamir spoke to everyone, and then he walked over to Riley. The room fell silent as everyone watched him walk to her bed. If looks could kill, he would have been dead fourteen times.

Mike stood up first and excused himself. He walked out of the room. Raelyn walked out after him, and then the rest of the ladies followed her. Riley's parents excused themselves and stepped out of the room after everyone else left. Jamir showing up had changed the energy at the hospital. Everyone had gone from excited to angry. Nobody was happy about it. Not even Riley.

Riley frowned, looked at Jamir, and then she asked, "What are you doing here?"

"I'm here to see my baby being born." Jamir replied.

"The last time I talked to you, you said fuck me and this baby." Riley said.

"I apologize. I was wrong. I was in the heat of the moment."

"I haven't even seen you this whole pregnancy and you show up here unannounced? I'm about to kick your ass up out of here. You're disrespectful. You don't even believe this baby is yours, and you played me in front of your wife like I was just a jump off. How the hell did you even find out that I was here?"

"Social media. Look, Riley my conscious was eating me up. I couldn't be out here with a baby that I know is mine, and not claim it, and not be a part of his or her life. I was on some bullshit with you and my wife, but I am here to right my wrongs, and ask you to allow me to be a part of my child's life. I would like to be here to witness my child being born. I want to be here for my baby. Please?"

"Wow Jamir. You really found an awkward time to show up."

"I know. You have me, and my wife blocked from your phone and social media, and I didn't want to just show up to your house after all that went down over there."

"Yea, and I have retraining orders on both of y'all."

"I know. I just decided to take my chances coming up here. My homeboy is still your friend on social media. He sent me a text message when you posted that it was time, and then he sent me a screen shot of your location. That is how I found out where you were."

Riley sucked her teeth and said, "Well, you know everyone up here is pissed. They do not want you here."

"I know."

She exhaled, closed her eyes, and then she opened them and said, "I'm still very mad at the way you handled me and our situation, but because this is your baby, so I will allow you to stay under two conditions. You have to be positive this whole delivery process even though my family wants to kill you, and you must promise to be in our child's life no matter what your wife feels about it."

"I promise."

"Ok."

"Can you tell my mom and dad to come here."

Jamir walked out of the room and told her parents that she wanted them to come back into the room. When they walked back in, she said, "Dad and mom this is Jamir.

He is my child's father. He is going to stay here for the delivery. I know that everyone is not going to be happy about it, but I want him here, so I'm asking that you and everyone else remain positive about this while I am giving birth to my first child."

Riley's mom and dad looked extremely irritated, but they agreed that they would do as she asked. Jamir walked over and formally introduced himself to them. Riley could see the frustration in her dad's face when he saw the wedding ring on Jamir's finger, but he didn't ask any questions. Riley asked them to tell everyone else to come back into the room, so her mom and dad stepped back out of the room to go and get everyone else. Riley looked at Jamir and shook her head.

Chapter 3

Raelyn

After Mike walked out of the room, I followed him. I wasn't going to stay in there and look at that fuck boy for another second. He had his nerve to show up to the hospital unannounced as far as I was concerned. I wanted to pull a Solange in the elevator and fuck him up.

I asked, "What the fuck is he doing here?"

"I don't know, but I was ready to snap." Cherry said.

"Me too." Taji said.

"Mike." I called out.

Mike stopped walking and let us catch up to him.

"Do you know what he is doing here?" I asked Mike.

"I don't." Mike replied.

"Oh hell no. I should go back in there and snap." I said angrily.

"Nah not here. Let's see what your sister wants to do." Mike said.

I let out a frustrated sound, "Uuuuggh." I grunted.

"Calm down. I'm mad too, but we need to stay calm for your sister, so she can have a safe delivery." he said.

"He's right." Cherry said.

I said, "I guess you're right. I will calm down for now, but if he says anything to me, I'm snapping."

The four of us sat in the lobby to wait and find out about what Riley was going to do about Jamir. Everyone was silent and in their own thoughts for a while. I was watching the news on the flat screen television up on the wall. I took my eyes off the television and looked around the room. I saw Mike stand up and walk over to the drink station to make another cup of coffee. Cherry and Paris were watching the television, and Taji was looking at her phone. My phone rang, but it was an unsaved number. I didn't recognize the number, so I ignored the call, and then I got a text message.

Hey Raelyn. It's Lamar. Please call me back when you can.

"Lamar?" I said out loud.

"What's wrong?" Paris asked.

"I don't know yet."

I wondered why Lamar would be calling me early in the morning. I tapped the screen to dial Lamar's number and call him back.

"Hey Lamar. Sorry that I didn't answer. I didn't know that it was you." I said.

"It's ok. Sorry to bother you but is Aleyah with you?" he asked.

"No, she isn't. Why? What's wrong?"

"Nothing, she just didn't come home last night. I tried calling her phone, but it's going straight to voicemail. I thought she was with you."

"No, the last time I saw her was in the club, and she was leaving out with Karina." I said.

"Alright. Well, if you talk to her, tell her to call me."

"Ok." I said. I frowned when I hung up.

"Is everything alright?" Paris asked.

"That was Aleyah's husband looking for her."

"Really?" Taji asked.

"He's never called me looking for her, but he said she didn't go home last night." I said.

"Oh boy." Taji said.

"I know right. I hope that she is alright." I said.

"Especially if she's been messing with Niko. I told y'all that dude is bat shit crazy." Taji said.

"I know. I don't even want to think like that. Anyways. I'm about to go and check on sis." I said.

My mom walked up right when I was standing up. "Riley asked for you guys to come back to the room." she said.

My mom had a look of irritation, but she was trying to remain calm and polite. Paris told me that she would wait in the lobby, so the rest of us walked with my mom back to the hospital room. Jamir was standing next to Riley's bed when we walked in. Riley waited for everyone to walk in, and then she started talking.

"Ok. I know that this is awkward for everyone, but this is my child's father, so he is going to stay for the delivery of my baby. I asked him, so I am going to ask you guys as well to please refrain from any negativity and try to get along for the birth of my child. I want all of you to be here, but if you don't want to be here, you can leave."

I saw Mike put his hands in his pockets and put his head down. Taji and Cherry were silent. They made their way to the other side of the room. I folded my arms and gave my sister an evil look.

"Raelyn." she said.

"Fine sister." I said, and then I looked at Jamir and cut my eyes.

Mike walked over to Riley and said, "I'm going to get out of here. Call me when your baby is here, ok?"

"Mike?" Riley looked at him with sad eyes.

"It's good, alright?" Mike said.

"Alright." Riley said,

"Alright Bruh." he said to Jamir before turning to walk out of the room.

"Alright everyone." Mike spoke to the rest of us. He waved as he made his way out of the room.

After Mike left, me and the ladies told Riley that we would be in the lobby. They stood up and followed me back out of the room. My mom and dad stayed in there with Riley.

Chapter 4

Eazy

I woke up New Year's Day to a stranger. Not only did I not know the female, but she looked totally different with her make-up off. She looked nothing like the beauty queen that I met in the club the night before. I moved my arm from around shorty's neck and sat up in the hotel bed. I picked up my phone and read a few text messages from my mom and sisters telling me that Riley's baby was on the way and everyone was at the hospital. I was in no rush to get to the hospital. I've done the labor and delivery thing with Karina and I know that it takes time for a baby to be born. My primary focus for the first day of the year was to get in touch with my baby's mother and check her ass. I was tired of the bullshit.

I woke shorty up and told her that we had to get out of there. After we got dressed, I told her that I would call her even though I had no plans to do so. I didn't even remember her name. As I was walking through the hotel to the parking ramp, I text message Raelyn to see how far along Riley was. Raelyn responded saying that she still wasn't dilated enough to give birth. I knew what that meant, so I called Karina. She answered the phone after the third ring.

"Yea. Where are you at?" I asked as I opened my car door to get in.

"At home." she said.

Her voice sounded groggy like I had just woken her up.

"I'm on my way." I said.

"On your way where?"

"Over there. See you in a few."

I hung up before she could respond. I drove over there ready for whatever. I didn't care if she had a dude over there or not. She was going to hear what I had to say, and if a dude was there, he could get it too. Karina didn't stay too far from the hotel that I was at, so I knew that I could get there quick. I sped through a couple of yellow lights, did a couple of stop and rolls at a few stop signs, and I made it to her house in under fifteen minutes. Karina answered the door in her pajamas. Her hair was in a messy bun on the top of her head, and she had no make-up on. She didn't look bad without make-up. She just looked tired. She was squinting her eyes because of the sun. I was sure that she was hung over.

"What the hell is your problem?" she asked.

"I should be asking you the same thing. I said angrily.

I pushed past her and stepped into her house. I saw her friend from the night before sitting on her couch watching television.

"Excuse me? I didn't say that you could come in." Karina said.

She closed the front door, and then she folded her arms and stood back on one of her legs.

I turned to look at her and said, "I don't give a fuck. I'm coming in anyway." I turned to her friend and said, "Hey miss. I don't know your name, but could you excuse us for a minute?"

"Sure." she said and stood up.

Karina rolled her eyes and said, "Shalita this is Eazy; Eazy, Shalita."

"Nice to meet you." Shalita said, and then she disappeared into one of the bedrooms on the first floor.

"New friend?" I asked.

"Actually, new roommate. Now, what do you want?" she asked.

"I've never known for you to have a roommate."

"I needed help with some of my bills, and she needed a place to stay. It worked out." she said.

She turned and walked to the kitchen. I followed her in there. She pulled her coffee pot from the machine, rinsed it, and then she started a fresh pot of coffee.

"You're hungover ain't you?" I asked.

"I am."

"I bet, and that is why I came over here. To talk to you about last night at the club."

"I was drunk, and your bitch was talking shit. What?"

"See that's what I'm talking about! She didn't say shit to you Karina! You started popping off for no reason! That shit is going to stop now!"

"If a bitch needs to be checked, I'ma check her!"

"Not on my muthafuckin watch and not at my event! You could have cost me money last night!"

"You weren't about to lose no money. Stop being dramatic." Karina rolled her eyes at me.

"I'm so fucking sick and tired of your attitude and disrespect! This is why the shit didn't work between us! Because you think you can do, say, or act however you want! You're never accountable for your actions!"

"So, you're really mad at me right now, but you had a whole bitch at your house while my daughter was there."

"See! That shit right there! Completely avoiding the topic so you can point the finger at me! This has nothing to do with that. This is about you thinking that you can come around and try to sabotage what I have going on! You're not doing that shit no more Karina! You're going to stay the fuck out of my business! Quit asking me to get back together because we're not! This shit is over with understand!? No more coming to my house! No more coming to my events turning up! No fucking more, and I'm not playing!"

"Whatever, Eazy."

I turned around, walked out, and slammed the door behind me. I got into my car and was about to pull off, but my phone started ringing. I pulled it out of my pocket to look at it thinking it better not be Karina trying to argue some more. It was an unsaved number. I usually didn't answer calls from numbers that I didn't know, but something told me to answer it that day. I thought that I was tripping when I heard the voice on the other end. I wasn't expecting to get a call from Aleyah on New Year's Day.

Chapter 5

Aleyah

Aleyah sat quietly in the car with Niko thinking of an escape plan. She had gone through many scenarios in her head, and not one of them seemed like they were going to work. She took her eyes off the naked trees going by, and turned her attention to the road signs, so she could try to figure out where she was. Niko was humming and tapping his fingers to a Rihanna song playing on the radio.

He stopped humming to ask, "Are you ok baby?"

Niko put his hand on her leg. He was acting like everything was normal. Like he hadn't kidnapped her, or like he hadn't smacked the crap out of her, or like he wasn't driving with a gun in his lap with the barrel facing her. Aleyah didn't respond. She was silent while looking at the road ahead. Niko continued to talk to her as if everything was normal.

"I know that you're probably hungry, we'll get some food soon baby, ok?"

Aleyah side eyed him. She looked at the gun in his lap and thought about trying to grab it to put it to his head and make him pull over, and then she thought about shooting him with it. Aleyah didn't think she could grab it fast enough, so she decided to stay quiet and pay attention to the road signs. She eventually saw a sign that said there was a certain number of miles left before they reached Chicago. Aleyah looked at the clock. It was eight o'clock in the morning on New Year's Day. She knew that Lamar was probably pissed off, or worried sick, or a little bit of both. Aleyah didn't know what she was going to tell him if she made it out of that situation

Aleyah still remained silent. They drove for a little while longer until they got to an exit that lead to a rest stop with gas stations and restaurants. He put his gun back into his waist band as he pulled the car off the exit. He slowly pulled his car into the first gas station and found an empty pump. Aleyah surveyed the area as they were pulling up. It was a huge rest stop with a lot of stores and restaurants. The gas station was full of people. It looked like a lot of people were traveling for the holiday. Aleyah spotted a Subway, a Pizza hut, a Taco Bell, Denny's, and there was Dunkin Donuts connected to the gas station they had pulled into.

"Don't try anything slick." Niko warned Aleyah before getting out of the car.

He locked the car doors after getting out. Aleyah looked around to see who was watching. She figured if she screamed and hollered maybe someone would help. Aleyah looked through the back window to see if Niko was watching her. She watched Niko put his credit card in the machine to pay for the gas at the pump. The card must not have been working because he made a frustrated sound and tried it again. She watched him press a couple of buttons, and then she heard him curse. She saw Niko look around, and then he walked back to the car.

He opened the driver's side door and said, "The child locks are on. You can't get out, so don't try it."

Niko closed the door and locked it with his key ring. Aleyah watched him walk into the store. She surveyed the scene again. The two cars next to theirs were empty, Pizza hut as too far away, but there was another entrance to the gas station. Aleyah decided to try her luck to get there. She knew that she had to move quickly She pulled her door handle a couple of times to see if he was bluffing, but it wouldn't open.

"Fuck!" she yelled and pounded the window a couple time to get someone's attention, but no one looked her way.

She quickly reached back to try the back door, but that one was locked too, and then she remembered that Niko opened his door from the inside. She looked back at the store to see if he was making his way back. When she didn't see him, she tried the door. It opened. She grabbed her car key out of his door handle and jumped out. She ran to the back of the car kneeled for a second, and then she ran across to the next car. She kneeled behind it, and then made her way to the next car. After the third car, she bolted to the other side of the gas station. She prayed that he didn't see her as she was entering the donut shop connected to the gas station. She kept her eyes scanning the store as she made her way to the bathroom. Aleyah was scared, her heart was beating fast and she could feel her hands shaking. She hurriedly walked into the bathroom and began looking around for an escape. Aleyah didn't know where she was. The only thing on her mind was getting away. She prayed that he wouldn't find her.

Chapter 6

Karina

Karina rolled her eyes when Eazy walked out of her house and slammed the door. In her mind, he had his nerve to be pissed off at her. He wouldn't have been pissed off, if he would have been with her at the New Year's Eve party instead of the chick that he was with. Karina didn't understand why he was trying to replace her with some whack female anyway. To her, she was his first and his always.

Eazy and Karina had lost their virginity to each other, so to her, Eazy could never love anyone else the way that he loved her. Karina cheated on him, but she blamed that on him. They had gotten into an argument and he told her that he was done. She didn't know that he was only speaking out of anger, so she messed with someone else. Karina felt like technically she didn't cheat, but he blew it up and everything went downhill from there. Suddenly, he hated everything she did and everything that he didn't like about her started to come out. He hated her attitude, and how she dressed. Karina felt like he was just trying to find reasons to not be together, but it was too late because she was already pregnant with their child.

Eazy made it a point to make sure that she understood that it was over. First, he moved out and moved back in with his parents, and then he started partying a lot before he became an events planner. He started posting pics on his social media page with other chicks he met at the club, and then he blocked her from his social media. Karina got on some petty stuff and started hating every time she seen him with someone knew; just like she did with Tiffani. In Karina's mind, If Eazy wasn't going to be hers, he wasn't going to be with anybody.

Karina poured hot coffee into her large bedazzled coffee mug. She added cream and sugar and stirred them in the hot liquid.

Shalita walked into the kitchen, and said, "He was mad."

"Girl, yea he was, but he can put some ice on that heat because I don't care."

"Do you blame him? I mean, you did act a fool last night." Shalita said.

Shalita poured coffee into a cup, stirred in creamer, and then she said, "You were so drunk that I had to damn near carry you in here."

Karina started laughing, "I wasn't that drunk."

"Yes, you were. Ask Aleyah. Both of us walked you to the car."

"Aleyah was there?"

"Yea, you don't remember?"

"No."

"See. I told you that you were drunk. We walked you to the car, and this was after you tried to pop Eazy's girl upside the head and hit Eazy with your earring. Security kicked us out, and then you were going off outside in the cold for fifteen minutes.

"Oh my gosh! I remember trying to fight the girl, and the only thing I remember after that was waking up to Eazy calling this morning."

"That's a damn shame." Shalita said.

Karina laughed.

"I don't understand why you be tripping on him like that, if you said you're done with him." Shalita said.

"I am done with him. I just didn't like the way the bitch looked at me."

"All that because a chick looked at you funny? I would hate to see you if she would have bumped into you or something."

"Bitch, I would've snatched that cheap ass wig off her head."

Shalita started laughing and shaking her head back and forth. She sat down at the dining room table with her cup of coffee.

"Are you hungry?" Karina asked.

"Hell yea."

"Good because I'm about to make my traditional first of the year breakfast."

"What's that?"

"Black eyed peas, corn bread, salmon croquets, and grits."

"That's about to be bomb."

"Hell yea." Karina said.

Karina turned around and started pulling things out of the cabinets and refrigerator. After she put some things on the counter, she heard her phone ringing. She walked to the living room to get it from the coffee table. She was surprised to see Lamar's number.

"Hey Brother. What's up?"

"Hey sis. Is Aleyah with you?"

"No. Uh-uh."

"Have you seen or talked to her?"

"No. Well, apparently not since last night, but I was so drunk that I don't remember. My friend told me that she was with us for a short time."

"Hmmmm." Lamar said.

"What's wrong?"

"She didn't come home last night."

"She didn't come home?" Karina asked.

"Nope."

Karina looked at the clock on her wall. It was almost nine-thirty in the morning. She asked, "Have you called her?"

"Yes, her phone keeps going to voicemail."

"I'm going to call her. I'll let you know if I talk to her brother."

"Ok."

Karina hung up and looked at the phone with a screwed up facial expression. Her first thought was Niko.

"I know this girl isn't laid up with Niko somewhere." she said to herself as she walked back into the kitchen.

"What's wrong?" Shalita asked.

"Aleyah didn't go home last night. That was her husband calling looking for her."

"Ah shit." Shalita said before taking a sip of her hot coffee.

"I know right." Karina said.

She tapped her phone screen to call Aleyah, but the call went straight to voicemail. She hung up and put the phone on the counter.

"I hope that she is ok."

Chapter 7

Aleyah

Aleyah was standing in the bathroom breathing hard and looking around for an escape. She didn't know how she was going to get out of there without Niko seeing her or finding her. She heard the door, so she jumped and prepared for battle, but it was an older African American woman. She looked like she was also traveling. She was short, round, and had grey hair in the front of her head, but the rest of her hair was black. She had her hair in loose curls and hanging on her shoulders. She was wearing a leather coat and boots, and she was carrying an oversized purse. Aleyah knew that she must have looked crazy because she was still wearing the dress and boots that she had on the night before. Aleyah turned to the sink and pretended to be washing her hands. She looked in the mirror. She saw that her make-up was partially worn off, and she had a bruise by her eye from when Niko smacked her in the car.

"Baby are you ok?" the woman asked.

"Yes." Aleyah said.

"Are you sure that you don't need some help? I saw you outside hiding behind my car and then running, so I thought that I would come in here and check on you. Did that man you are with do something to you?"

Aleyah felt tears filling up in her eyes, she said, "I've been kidnapped."

"By that man you pulled up with?"

"Yes."

"Yea he was just out there looking for you. Do you want to call the police?"

"No, I don't. I just need to get out of here and get home. He kidnapped me from Minnesota last night and drove me here. He has my purse and phone. He also has a gun."

"Child, I knew that something was wrong. Do you want my help? I'm going to Wisconsin. You can ride with me. Is there someone that you can call to meet you there?"

"I do not have any numbers memorized, but I have my credit card and my ID in my bra. I can figure something out once I get there."

"Ok. Go in one of those stalls and hide. Don't come out until I come and get you. I'ma pull my car around to this side of the store, so he doesn't see you get in, ok?"

Aleyah nodded her head.

"Go ahead baby." the woman said.

Aleyah walked quickly to the bathroom stall next to the last. She closed and locked the door, stood on the toilet seat, and bent down. She heard a bunch of people walk in with some kids, and then she heard Niko's voice.

"Aleyah!" he called into the bathroom. "Aleyah!" he repeated.

"There isn't anyone in here by that name sir." one of the ladies said.

"There isn't anyone else in here?" he asked.

"No there isn't." the other lady said.

"Alright, sorry about that." Niko said.

He walked away from the restroom, and back into the store. He searched the store again, and then he walked outside. The older black lady that was in the bathroom with Aleyah had just left the register and walked out behind him.

"Hey son. Are you looking for that girl that you pulled up with? With the long black hair?"

"Yes. Have you seen her?"

"Yes. I saw her run across the street to that Pizza Hut. She was running fast too. Is everything ok?"

"Yes, ma'am that's my wife. She has some mental problems. She is always disappearing, and then I have to go and find her."

The lady laughed and said, "My ex-husband used to do the same thing. That's why we're not married now. Well, you better go get her before she gets lost out here."

Niko laughed and thanked the lady. He walked to his car, and then the lady walked to hers. She saw him pull off and head towards the Pizza Hut. She quickly started her car and pulled it around to the other side of the gas station.

She got out and walked back inside to the bathroom. Aleyah heard her knock on the bathroom stall door.

"You can come out now sweetie, but we have to go fast because he might be back."

"Ok. Thank you so much." Aleyah said.

They snuck out of the bathroom, and then Aleyah followed her out of the store to her car. They got in and the lady pulled out. Aleyah leaned her seat all the way back until she was practically laying down.

"I hope that you like chips, pop, and a sandwich. I got it for you because I figured that you would be hungry.

"I do. Thank you." Aleyah responded.

"Look friend, he is going back to the store looking for you. Just like I said." she said while looking through the rearview mirror.

Aleyah looked through hers and saw Niko's car driving from the Pizza Hut restaurant back to the gas station.

"I usually don't make a habit of picking up strangers, but you seemed like you needed some help.

What's your name, child?" the lady asked as she drove onto the highway entrance.

"Aleyah."

"Like the singer?"

"Yes, but it's spelled different."

"How is it spelled?"

"A-L-E-Y-A-H."

"Oh, that's different, but pretty."

"Thank you."

"My name is Carol, but everyone calls me Mama Carol."

"Nice to meet you Mama Carol."

"Nice to meet you too. I hope that you don't mind Gospel music."

"I love it."

Mama Carol turned her radio on and a song by Kirk Franklin began playing through the speakers. Aleyah looked out the rearview mirror to make sure Niko wasn't following them. She was still shaken by the whole ordeal.

"Now tell me how a young and beautiful young lady like yourself ended up getting kidnapped. Did you know that guy?"

"I do. He was my friend."

Mama Carol looked down at Aleyah's hand.

"Looks like you're married."

"I am."

"Does your husband know about this friend?"

"Kind of."

"Boy I tell you. You young girls these days. You've got to be careful who your calling friends, and who you are dealing with. These young people aren't holding all their marbles."

"I know. I should have cut it off a long time ago, but I didn't, and I woke up in his car this morning on the way to Virginia. My husband doesn't even know where I am."

"Yea that's unfortunate. Well, I'm glad you're safe now."

"Do you think that he is going to come looking for you when you get home?"

"I'm pretty sure that he will."

"You might want to call the police dear when you get back and get him arrested, or he might hurt you, and I would hate for that to happen to someone as beautiful as you."

"You're right."

"Have you figured out someone to call yet? Do you know your husbands' number or your mom?"

"I'm so used to just dialing numbers that are already saved in my phone. I can't remember any." Aleyah said.

She began wrecking her brain to think of a number. She couldn't think of Karina's number or the twins, and then suddenly a number popped into her head. She couldn't believe that she still remembered it, but Eazy hadn't changed his number since high school.

"I think that I remembered a number for a friend of mine."

"Here's my phone. Try calling it."

Aleyah dialed Eazy's number. It rang a couple of times and then he answered.

"Eazy."

"Aleyah?"

"Yes."

"Whose number is this?"

"It's Mama Carol's number. Listen, this is an emergency. I need your help. I really hope you can help me Eazy. I got stranded in Chicago, and I'm getting a ride to Wisconsin, but I need someone to meet me in Wisconsin to pick me up to get me back to Minnesota. I don't have my car, my purse, or my phone. I don't have anything. Your number is the only number that I have. I need you to meet me in Wisconsin to pick me up please."

"Chicago? What? What the hell is going on Aleyah? How did you end up there?"

"It's a long story Eazy and I can't go through it right now. I really need you to come and meet me please."

"Alright. Whatever you need."

"Oh my God! Thank you so much! I'm going to give the phone to Mama Carol, so she can tell you where to meet us."

Aleyah handed Mama Carol the phone. She listened to her tell Eazy about a large rest stop in Wisconsin that he should meet them. She told him that it would take them four hours to get there. Eazy told her that he would be there, and then she hung up the phone.

Mama Carol said, "He sounds like a nice guy."

"He is."

"I'm glad someone can meet you. I was going to be worried about you."

"That's really sweet. This was nice of you to do this for me."

"It's no problem. Sometimes God puts us in places for a reason. I wasn't even going to stop at that rest stop. I was going to keep going until the next one. Lucky for you that I did decide to stop."

"Yes, it was. What are you going to Wisconsin for?"

"I live in Wisconsin. I was in Chicago visiting family for the Holidays."

"Oh ok."

"Well honey we've got a drive ahead of us, so just sit back and relax. You're safe now."

Aleyah knew that lady was heaven sent. She said a silent prayer thanking God for saving her.

Chapter 8

Riley

Riley was ready to give up. She had pushed so many times, and her baby had not come out. She was exhausted, in pain, and ready for it to be over. Riley looked around the room. The doctor and the nurse were at the foot of the bed. Jamir was standing on the side watching the doctor deliver their baby. Riley's mom was on one side of her bed holding her hand and Raelyn was on the other side.

Riley looked at her mom and said, "I can't mom."

"Yes, you can baby. Just breath. She is almost here." her mom said.

"You got it sister. You're doing great." Raelyn said.

The doctor said, "Ok Riley. All you need is just one more good push and your daughter will be here."

Riley shook her head back and forth. She didn't want to push any more.

"I can't." she said.

"It's ok. Baby you can do it." her mom said.

Everyone in the room including Jamir chimed in giving Riley encouragement. Jamir touched her leg and Raelyn grabbed her other hand, although she wanted to kick Jamir for even touching her, she appreciated the support from him. Riley looked around at everyone again, and then she agreed that she was going to do it.

The doctor said, "Ok. I'm going to count to three and then I want you to push as hard as you can."

The doctor counted to three, and then Riley took a deep breath and gave one last hard push. She heard the doctor tell her that she was doing good. She heard her mom say that she could see the baby's hair. She heard Jamir tell her that their baby was coming, and then she felt the baby slide out. Everyone in the room began cheering when they saw the baby in the doctor's hands. Riley started crying when she heard her baby's first cry. Riley's mom and sister's eyes filled with tears.

"You did good baby." their mom said.

"You did sister." Raelyn said as she wiped her tears.

The doctor and nurse moved quickly to clean the baby up, weigh her, and swaddle her.

"Six pounds and two ounces." the nurse called out.

"The doctor handed the swaddled baby girl to Riley and said, "Congrats mom and dad and Happy New Year."

Riley looked down at her new baby girl in her arms. She was in awe at how beautiful she was. She had wondered the entire nine months what her baby was going to look like and she could finally see her and hold her.

"She is so beautiful." Riley said.

"She is. Just like her mom and grandma." her mother said.

Raelyn and their mom cooed over the baby, and then they stepped out of the room to tell everyone else that the baby had arrived, and to let the nurses clean Riley up.

"Do you want to hold her?" Riley asked.

Jamir scooped the baby into his arms and looked at her.

"Wow. She is beautiful Riley. Just like you. Wow. Look at my daughter. My first daughter. Thank you."

Riley smiled at him, and then Jamir said, "I'm sorry for everything. I really am."

"Thank you."

"I promise I'm gonna be here and take care of my baby. No matter what."

"Do you really mean that?"

"On God. Ain't nothing going to hold me back from my baby girl." he said while staring at the baby. He looked at Riley and said, "Thank you."

The nurses finished cleaning Riley up and congratulated her and Jamir. They told her that they would be back. Jamir leaned down to kiss Riley, and then Raelyn and the rest of the family walked back into the room with balloons and gifts.

Chapter 9

Eazy

I didn't know what Aleyah had gotten herself into. "Chicago?" I kept saying that to myself. I couldn't figure out how she ended up in Chicago after leaving the New Year's Eve party the night before. I went through several scenarios in my head as I made my way to the hospital to meet my new niece. I had a few hours before I needed to drive to Wisconsin to meet and pick up Aleyah, so I stopped by the hospital to celebrate the new edition to our family. I made it to the hospital just in time for the delivery, and I was pissed to find out that the fuck boy was there. I wanted to put hands on him for doing my sister dirty, but my dad told me to chill.

I waited in the hallway with my dad, my sister's, friends, and my cousin. I was anxious the entire time worrying about Aleyah. I didn't tell anyone that I had talked to her because I wanted to find out the full story first. I checked my phone a few times to make sure she hadn't tried to call me again with new or different instructions. Eventually, Raelyn and our mom emerged from the delivery room to tell everyone that the baby was born. My mom said that she was beautiful and healthy with all ten fingers and ten toes. She told us the baby's weight, and then she told us that we had to wait to for a moment, so the doctor and nurse could get Riley cleaned up.

As we were waiting Raelyn asked me, "Have you talked to Aleyah bro?"

"Nah. Why?"

"Because her husband has called me a couple of times looking for her."

"Oh yea?"

"Yup. He called this morning, and then he called again not too long ago. I hope everything is alright with her. I tried to call her, but I got her voicemail."

"Wow. Yea. I'm sure that she is ok sis. Don't worry. I'll see if I can get in touch with her when I leave here." I said.

The doctor walked out of the room and told everyone that they could go in and meet the baby. Everyone picked up their gifts and balloons and walked into the room to see Riley and my new niece.

Chapter 10

Aleyah

Aleyah stayed up the entire ride with Mama Carol chatting about life and current news. During the ride she had learned that Mama Carol had four kids and seven grandchildren. Her kids were all Aleyah's age and older. Her oldest son was in prison and had been for ten years. Her oldest daughter was battling a drug addiction and was in the process of cleaning her life up. Mama Carol was happy that she was changing her life. Her youngest daughter was doing well for herself. She was a nurse and she helped Mama Carol take care of her two older siblings' kids. Mama Carol was most proud of her youngest son who plays for the NFL. She said that he played for the Chicago

Bears, and that was the reason she was there visiting and bringing in the New Year with him and other family.

"Why didn't he fly you out there?" Aleyah asked.

"Oh Chile, I hate planes and the airport. I love to drive, and it's only a four to five-hour drive anyways. He can give me that money, so I can put it in my gas tank. The amount of time that it takes to get to the airport, through security, and on the plane; I could be half way there on the road."

Aleyah laughed and said, "I understand."

Aleyah looked out of the window at all the naked trees and snow passing them by and asked herself how she let the situation with Niko go that far. Guilt was setting in big time and she still hadn't figured out how she was going to explain where she'd been to Lamar. Mama Carol looked down at the ring on Aleyah's left hand again.

"So, you're married, and your friend kidnapped you?" she asked.

"Yes ma'am."

"Chile that's some mess there."

"I know." Aleyah said. She looked down at the ring on her finger.

"Listen, I know that you feel bad right now, but pray about it. God will forgive you and deliver you."

"Thank you."

"We've all done bad. Ain't nobody perfect in this world."

"You're right."

"He spared you your life today. Who knows what the crazy fool was planning to do. Just ask God for forgiveness."

Aleyah smiled and nodded her head. Mama Carol gave Aleyah her phone to call Eazy to make sure he was still going to meet her at the rest stop. Eazy said that he was already there waiting for her. Aleyah was relieved and told him that they were pulling up. She gave him the color of the car she was in. She hung up and gave the phone back to Mama Carol. They pulled off the exit and followed the road signs to the rest stop.

"Well this is it. Are you sure that you are safe with him?"

"Yes. I am."

"Good. My daughter was in the streets bad, and her pimp kidnapped her once. You don't know the heartache I felt when she was missing. You reminded me of her. I guess that's why I helped. I know that you're not on drugs, but I'm sure your dealing with your own struggles. Keep God in your life and he will show you the way." Mama Carol said as they pulled up to a gas pump and parked.

Aleyah spotted Eazy's car parked backwards in a parking spot. She pointed at the car and told Mama Carol that was her ride. Tears started falling from Aleyah's eyes. "Thank you so much Mama Carol. You saved my life."

"Oh honey. It was no problem at all. I'm just glad you're safe. Don't cry baby."

Aleyah reached out and hugged Mama Carol. Mama Carol hugged her tight.

"Stop crying. You take care of yourself and your child. I want you to take this card. It has my number on it. I'm a pastor at a church. If you need anything. I mean anything. You make sure that you call me."

"I will."

"Also, call me to let me know that you made it home. Stay out of trouble and stay away from those bad guys ok?"

"Yes ma'am."

"Maybe you can come up for a holiday with your son and spend time with my family and grandkids."

"That's a plan Mama Carol."

"Alright, well, bye baby. It was great to meet you."

"Bye Mama Carol. Thank you again."

"No problem sweetie."

Aleyah got out of Mama Carol's car and walked over to Eazy's car. She waved at Mama Carol before getting inside. Mama Carol waved back, and then Aleyah got into Eazy's car. They pulled out of the gas station. Aleyah watched Mama Carol pull out of the gas station behind them. She turned a different direction than them. Mama Carol told her that she lived ten minutes from the rest stop, so Aleyah figured that she was heading home. She said a silent prayer thanking God again for sending Mama Carol her way.

Chapter 11

Eazy

Aleyah got into my car and hugged me. She was looking and smelling like she'd been out all night. I'd never seen Aleyah looking bad. Her make-up was worn off, and she still had on the clothes that she was wearing the night before. That was not typical behavior from Aleyah. She was a woman that stayed clean and well put together. I surveyed her as I pulled out of the parking spot of the gas station.

"Are you ok?" I asked.

"Yea." she said as she sat back and put her seat belt on.

"Is that a bruise on your face?" I asked.

"Yes."

"What the hell is going on Aleyah? You get in here with the clothes you had on last night and coming from Chicago. You got me driving all the way to Wisconsin to meet with you. What's up?"

She rubbed her eyes and said, "It's such a long story Eazy. I'm just so happy you came."

"I'm not trying to hear that it's a long story shit Aleyah. You've been gone all night, and your husband has been calling around looking for you, so I know that you didn't go to Chicago with him. What's up?" I asked again with more aggression.

"Lamar was looking for me?" she asked.

"Yup. All day. He called my sisters, Karina, and he even called me. You know your husband can't stand me, so he must be worried, or pissed, or both."

"What did you tell him?" she asked nervously.

"I told him that I hadn't talked to you."

"Oh, thank God." she exhaled.

"So, tell me what's up. Were you with another dude or what?"

She paused and shook her head.

"Now, Aleyah." I said angrily.

"I was kidnapped."

"Kidnapped!? Who the hell gets abducted in the millennium Aleyah? Is that the lie that you're going to tell Lamar? Because it's not believable." I said.

"No, I'm serious Eazy." Aleyah said.

"You got kidnapped for real?" I asked.

"Yes. From the club last night." Aleyah said.

"Ah hell nah." I said angrily. "By a stranger?" I asked.

"No."

"You knew the person?" I asked.

"Yes."

"Who the fuck was it, so I can handle that muthafucka!" I said angrily.

"It's not that simple."

"The hell are you talking about? Let me know who it is so I can handle that shit for real!"

She broke down and started crying. "It's my fault Eazy."

"What do you mean it's your fault Aleyah?"

She wouldn't stop crying. I listened to her for a moment, and then I put my hand on her back.

"I'm sorry for my anger. I'm just worked up. You scared the shit out of me. I was worried, and so many things ran through my mind since I talked to you earlier. I shouldn't be yelling because I know that you have to deal with your husband soon, but you've got to talk to me and tell me what happened, so I'll know if and how I need to help you."

"You can't help me Eazy because I fucked up." she said.

She looked up at me with tears in her eyes and said, "I was having an affair. The person who abducted me is the person that I was having an affair with. He was my husband's best friend. He wanted me to leave Lamar to be with him, so he abducted me. He said that he was taking me to Virginia to hold me hostage and marry me."

I was frozen and speechless. I didn't know what to say. Aleyah had dropped too many bombs on me, so I was silent for a few minutes staring at the road in front of me while listening to her sniffle and cry.

I finally managed to say, "Whoa Aleyah. That's some shit."

"I know. I fucked up, and I'm scared."

"I have a question, and don't lie to me. Was it the dude that was at the club?"

"Yes." she said. More tears fell from her eyes.

"I knew something was up with you and that dude."

I shook my head and fell silent for a minute. I listened to her sniffle and cry, and then I said, "Stop crying Aleyah. Yea you fucked up, but it is what it is. You need to figure out what you're going to do because I'm sure dude ain't going to let you go that easy. Just judging by the way, he was acting at the club. What are you going to tell your husband?"

"I don't know yet."

"Wow."

I shook my head again. She cried for a little while and I rubbed her back, and then she dried her eyes and sat silently for the rest of the ride. When we reached Minneapolis, she asked if I could take her to her car. I pulled up to her car in the parking ramp and parked.

"Please don't tell anyone what happened. I will tell them when I figure things out."

I put my hands up and said, "I got you. I'm just glad that you're ok. Do you need me to follow you?"

"No."

"Are you sure?"

"Yes."

"Alright. You don't have a phone, so how will I know that you made it home safe?"

"I'm going to stop and get a new phone before I go home. I have my credit card on me."

"Alright, well, let me know that you got home safe and keep me posted on what happens with your husband. If you need somewhere to stay you know that you can come to my house. Also, text or call my sister when you get a chance. She had the baby today."

"Oh wow. Really?"

"Yea. I'm sure that she would be happy to hear from you."

"Ok. Thank you." she said.

"I'm going to follow you half way to make sure dude isn't lurking. Is that ok?"

"Yes, thank you so much Eazy. I love you."

"I love you too."

She hugged me tight, and then she got out of my car. I waited until she got into her car and pulled out, and then I followed her out of the parking ramp.

Chapter 12

Aleyah

"Where the fuck have you been all night!?" Lamar yelled when Aleyah walked into their house. "We need to talk."

"You're damn right we need to talk! It's almost four o'clock in the evening and you're just now walking into this house! I've been calling everyone looking for you!"

"I know Lamar."

"Nobody knew where you were, you weren't answering your phone, and you walk up in here looking crazy, and why the hell is your face bruised!?"

"Why is your lip busted?" Aleyah asked.

"Answer the question. Where were you?" Lamar said angrily.

Aleyah exhaled and said, "I was in Chicago."

"Chicago? What the hell were you doing all the way in Illinois?"

Aleyah exhaled again. She decided to just tell him the truth, so she said, "Um, Niko kidnapped me."

"Niko?"

"We've been having an affair."

"Wait. You've been messing around with my best friend?"

"Yes."

He dropped his head into his hands, and then he exploded, "The fuck Aleyah!"

Aleyah started crying, "I know. I fucked up and I'm sorry."

"Why Aleyah?!"

"I fucked up Lamar, and it's all bad. He started stalking me and threatening me to tell you if I didn't leave you for him, so I cut him off, and then he kidnapped me. He said he was taking me to Virginia. I escaped in Chicago."

"Oh my God." Lamar said as he was shaking his head side to side.

"That's why no one could get in touch with me because my phone was dead. The first time I tried to get a way he hit me and pulled a gun on me. He said that he was going to put me in the ground with his wife. That's how I got this bruise. I was so scared. I thought that I was going to die." Aleyah said through tears.

Lamar was so mad, he wanted to choke Aleyah.

"I'm fucking pissed at you right now!"

"I know."

"I knew something was going on, but I couldn't put my finger on it until he came over here drunk last night talking shit with my people here."

"What?"

"Yea he came over here talking crazy. Talking about he might be fucking you and he could take you from me. I put hands on him last night. That's how my lip got busted."

"Y'all got into a fight?"

"Hell yea! Tore the garage up. My friend and my cousin had to break it up, and I was trying to call you to ask you about what he was talking about, but you weren't answering the phone. Now I know why."

"Oh, my goodness."

"Hell yea. At first, I was pissed, and then I got worried, so I started calling everyone. I even called his punk ass. When he didn't answer, all kinds of stuff started going through my mind. I started thinking like maybe he wasn't just talking out of the side of his neck, and here you are telling me that he wasn't? What the fuck Aleyah!" he turned away from her and started pacing back and forth.

"I know Lamar. I'm sorry."

"I don't want to hear your sorry's right now." Lamar said.

He kept pacing while Aleyah's tears continued to fall. A million things going through his mind. He shook his head a few times, and then he stopped walking.

"How the hell did you get back here from Chicago anyways?"

"I called Eazy."

"Eazy? You called that muthafucka out of all people."

"He was the only number I had memorized."

"You trying to tell me that you don't have your husbands' number, or your mom's number memorized, but you got a dude number that you had feelings for memorized?"

"Lamar his number hasn't changed since high school. How many times have you and mom changed y'all numbers? It was the only number I could remember."

"Man, I can't believe you Aleyah."

"I know."

"Stop saying you know."

"I don't know what else to say."

"Tell me why you did the shit."

"I just got caught up."

"You just got caught up? Is that right? Now, this muthafucka Niko is probably on his way back here looking for you. I hope he shows up too, so I can whoop his ass again. Dumb as muthafucka."

"I called the police before I got here. They are on their way now."

"How did you do that with no phone?"

"I stopped to get a new one. Thank God a store was open."

"Why didn't you call me when you got your new phone?"

"Because I wanted to tell you the truth face to face instead of over the phone."

Lamar exhaled and said, "I can't even look at you right now." Lamar turned away from Aleyah and punched a hole in the wall.

"All I can say is I'm sorry babe, and I understand if you want to get a divorce." Aleyah said, and then the doorbell rang.

"You're damn right we're getting a divorce." Lamar said as he walked to the door to answer it. He opened the door to two police officers.

"Hello Sir, we are responding to a call." the female cop said.

"Yes, my wife called." Lamar said.

He stepped out of the way, so the officers could walk in. Lamar walked over to the dining room table and sat down in one of the chairs.

The female officer pulled out a note pad and pen. "So, we were informed that there was a kidnapping?" she asked Aleyah.

"Aleyah replied, "Yes." she heard Lamar exhale, and then she saw him shake his head and look down at the table.

"Were you abducted?"

"Yes. Last night."

"Was it a stranger, or did you know the person?"

"Um, he is a friend." Aleyah said, and then she heard Lamar say, "Um, um, um."

Lamar put his head in his hands and continued to look at the table.

"Can you please give us a description of what happened ma'am?"

"Um, yes, I was leaving the club last night."

"About what time?"

"One o'clock a.m. I was getting into my car, and he grabbed me from behind. He suffocated me until I passed out, and when I woke up this morning, I was in his car with him and we were on our way to Chicago. He said that he was taking me to Virginia to get married. When I demanded that he let me go, he hit me, and that is how I got this bruise. He also, pulled a gun on me, and told me that he would put me in the ground with his wife, if I tried to get away."

The police officer was silent while she wrote down what Aleyah told her. The officer finished writing and then asked, "So, he's armed?"

"Yes."

"Do you know what kind of firearm it is?"

"I don't."

"Was it a handgun?"

"Yes."

"Ok." The officer said while writing down some more things.

She stopped writing and asked, "Was there some kind of romantic involvement between you and him?"

"Yes."

Lamar exhaled loudly again, and said, "Oh my God."

"Sir, did you know anything about this?"

"No, I did not. I'm just finding out now." Lamar said angrily.

The officer asked Aleyah, "Do you know where he's at now?"

"No. I escaped in Chicago while we were getting gas and hitched a ride back. He still has my purse and my phone."

"Can you give us a description of what he looks like and what kind of vehicle he is driving?"

Aleyah gave them a description of Niko and his car. The officer took down the information, and then she put her notepad and pen into her back pocket. She told Aleyah that they needed to take a few pics of the bruise on her face.

Once they were finished taking pictures, the officer said, "I'm very sorry that this happened to you. We are going to canvas this area before we leave to make sure that he isn't around here. We strongly urge that you get a restraining order against him immediately. You might want to go and stay somewhere else like possibly with a friend or with family for a couple of days just in case he comes here looking for you."

"Ok."

"Call 911 immediately, if you see him, or if something happens."

"Ok."

"You folks have a good night."

The cops walked out of their house and Aleyah shut the door.

Lamar said, "I'm going to my sister's house. I need a few days away from you."

"Alright. I'm going to Karina's"

"Do what you want. Just call your mom, and the twins and tell them that you are ok."

"Ok. Can we please keep this to ourselves for now?"

"Whatever."

Aleyah and Lamar packed overnight bags and left their house. Lamar went to his sisters where their little man was, and Aleyah headed to Karina's. She called Mama Carol on her way there to tell her that she had made it home safe.

Chapter 13

Karina

Karina walked into her living room and plopped down on the couch next to Shalita. Shalita was watching New Year's Eve celebration recap on the news. The news anchors were talking about all the celebrity parties, performances, and fashion from the night before. Shalita set the remote on the coffee table and turned her attention to Karina.

"Aleyah just called. I guess her husband found her which is good, but she is coming to stay here for a few days."

"That's not a good sign." Shalita said.

"No, it's not."

"I'm anxious to find out what's going on." Shalita said.

"Yea. I hope everything is ok."

"I don't know her that well, but I do too."

"Anyways. My mom is on her way to drop Princess off, and Eazy text me to tell me that his sister had her baby today." Karina said.

"This year is starting off quite eventful."

"Yes, it is girl. I need to go up to the hospital to see the baby, but I wanna see what's going on with my bestie first."

Karina turned her attention to the television when she heard them say something about Rihanna. Rihanna, one of her favorite singers, was trending for something she wore to a New Year's Eve party.

"She's always killing it."

"All the time."

The doorbell rang, and Karina got up to answer the door.

"Hey girl." Karina said.

She hugged Aleyah, and then she saw the huge bruise by her eye.

"What the hell happened to you? Did Lamar put his hands on you? I will fuck Lamar up." Karina said furiously.

"No, girl, calm down. It's a long story. I just need a drink and to sit down."

"Come on. Give me your bags." Karina said.

Karina took Aleyah's bags to her guest bedroom on the second level. Aleyah walked into the living room and spoke to Shalita.

"Hey girl." Aleyah said to Shalita.

Shalita's eyebrows went up when she saw Aleyah's bruise. "Oh my gosh. What happened?" Shalita asked.

"Girl." Aleyah said when she sat down in the lazy boy chair.

Karina walked back down the stairs and into the living room, and then she said, "Oh. I should tell you that Shalita is rooming with me now, so don't be surprised to see her in the morning."

"Well y'all might have to make room for me."

"Ok. This sounds like a wine situation." Karina said as she walked towards the kitchen.

"It's a hard liquor situation."

"Oh shit. I'll get the bottle of Patron out and mix us up some drinks."

Karina moved quickly getting cups, filling them with ice, pouring double shots of patron in each one, and mixing in a little juice. She walked back into the living room and handed both Shalita and Aleyah cups of the alcoholic beverage that she had made.

"Let's toast to the New Year first."

They tapped cups together, and then swallowed down a gulp of their drinks.

"Ok now what happened? Because Lamar called me twice today, and you were nowhere to be found, and I didn't know what to tell him."

Aleyah exhaled, shook her head, and said, "Girl, so after we left the club last night. I was abducted."

"What!?" Karina asked.

"Whoa. That's serious." Shalita said.

"Wait. Kidnapped? Who the fuck kidnaps people in the millennium?" Karina asked.

"Apparently Niko." Aleyah said.

"Fine ass Niko?" Karina asked.

"Yup."

"Fine ass Niko kidnapped you?" Karina asked.

"Yup."

"Whoa." Shalita said before taking a sip of her drink.

"He knocked me out. I think he used something because I kind of remember him putting something over my face, and like a sweet smell, but I don't remember. It happened so fast, and it's so fuzzy. All I know is, I couldn't breathe, and then I blacked out. I woke up this morning in the car with him telling me that we were on the way to Virginia."

"Shut up best friend."

"Seriously. No lies."

"Oh my God." Shalita said.

Aleyah's eyes began to water, and then she caught a tear with her finger.

"Oh my God. That muthafucka is crazy as hell. I can't believe he did that shit." Karina said.

"Yea girl. He did. I was so scared. I tried to fight, but he hit me. That's how I ended up with this bruise on my face, and then he pulled a gun on me. I was for sure that I was going to die. By the grace of God, we had to stop to get gas, and that's how I escaped. I jumped out of the car and ran. This older black lady saw me and helped me. He has my purse and phone. I had nothing. The only number I could remember was Eazy's. He met me in Wisconsin and brought me back here."

Karina put her cup down, stood up, and walked over to sit next to Aleyah. She wrapped her arms around Aleyah and hugged her. Shalita did the same. Aleyah cried for a little while, and then she dried her eyes.

"I knew that I was messing up when I was doing it, but I wasn't expecting all this to happen."

"I wouldn't have expected it either. The most I would have worried about is my husband finding out."

"Yea, well, I told him, and he wants a divorce. I expected that."

"Yea? I'm sorry."

"It's ok."

"What about Niko? Did you call the police?" Karina said.

"Niko is still on the loose, and the police are looking for him. They told me and Lamar to hide out for a few days."

"This is too much." Karina said.

"Are you sure that he didn't follow you here?" Shalita asked.

"I don't think so." Aleyah said.

"We should put her car in the garage." Shalita said to Karina.

"Yep, we should. Let's go. Let me get your keys best friend." Karina said.

Aleyah handed Karina her car keys. Karina grabbed the keys, and then her and Shalita walked outside to move Shalita's car out of the garage and put Aleyah's car in it.

Karina had decided to skip the hospital, so she could stay with her friend. The new year had started off with more excitement and surprises than she had planned for.

***

"Ah! right there!" Karina whined. Karina's body convulsed a few times before she moaned, "Oh my goodness babe."

"Shhhh. Be quiet before your best friend hears us, and I know you don't want that."

"I'm sorry babe. It just feels so good." Karina said.

"I know. I like it when you cum."

Karina smiled and said, "I love you."

"Do you love me for real?" Shalita asked.

"Yes, baby I do."

"Well, when are we going to let it be known. When are we going to tell people about us?" Shalita said as she laid next to Karina.

"It's not that simple." Karina said.

"I'm tired of being your secret."

"You're not."

"Why ain't I? Nobody knows. You're out here running around after your ex, but you're fucking me on the low while I'm playing the roommate role. I thought that you said that you were over him."

"I am over him."

"I can't tell."

"Baby, stop. You know that I love you, and you know it's not that easy. There's a lot that goes into us going public."

"It's easier than living this lie Karina. You move me in here. I'm playing auntie to your daughter. I'm fake sleeping in another room, but I'm sneaking in here at night, and then leaving here early in the morning before Princess wakes up. On top of that, I gotta play cool in front of your friends and act like I'm alright with listening to you talk about your baby daddy all the time. I'm tired of that. I'm ready for everyone to know that we are together."

"I'm not ready yet Shalita."

"When will you be ready?"

"I don't know."

Shalita laid down next to her and turned her back towards her.

"Baby don't be like that. We will let people know when the time is right." Karina said.

"When will it be right? Twenty years from now? I'm telling you now, I'm not going to be the fake best friend that you bring to your family's Thanksgiving dinner every year for the next fifteen years."

"You know that my family is heavy in the church. I don't know how they would react to me being like this."

"Like what? A lesbian? Say it."

"It's new to me."

"I'm aright with who I am. Why can't you be?"

"Because it's new to me and I'm not ready yet. I don't know how I'm going to explain to my daughter that she is going to have two mommies."

"Be honest."

"Baby just give it time ok?"

"Alright fine."

"Come here." Karina said.

Shalita turned around. She curled up with Karina and they fell asleep. Per usual, she got up before dawn, and crept back upstairs to her room.

Chapter 14

Riley

Riley's parents drove Riley and her new baby home from the hospital. Mike met them outside to help them get, Riley, the baby, and their things into the house. Riley was happy to be out of the hospital and in the comfort of her own home. Riley's mom asked Riley if she wanted her to stay with her and the baby, but Riley told her that Mike was there, and Cherry had planned to be over in a little while.

"Ok. Call me if you need anything."

"I will."

Her mom kissed her new grandbaby on the forehead and said, "Take care of my daughter and my grandbaby."

"Yes ma'am. I will. I promise." Mike said.

She hugged him and walked out. Riley's mom had taken a liking to Mike after spending some time with him at the hospital.

Welcome home." Mike said.

"Thank you."

"Where's your boy?" Mike asked.

"Oh, he was up there today, but he left after I was released." Riley said.

"I'm not going to lie to you. I was pissed when I saw him walk into your room."

"I know. Everyone was."

"I had to go after you said that you wanted him to stay. What was up with that Ri?"

"I don't know. I just felt that it was right. I mean she is his baby."

"Yea, but that dude wasn't around your entire pregnancy. He told you fuck you and the baby. I just don't understand why you felt that he deserved that after how he treated you."

"I wanted to be angry with him, but honestly I was kind of relieved that he stepped up. I mean, it was pretty brave of him to walk up in there with all my family and friends unexpected."

"He was definitely stepping into some fire. Your sister was ready to snap. I had to calm her down."

"I know she was. I was ready to snap too, but I knew that I needed to stay calm while I was trying to bring life into the world."

"I hear you."

"Thank you for coming back up there."

"It ain't no problem. I just needed to step away to calm down." he said, and then he looked at the baby in the car seat and said, "She is beautiful. Tell me her name again."

"Raina Marie."

"I see you stuck with the R's like you and your sister."

"Yea. I gave her my mom's middle name."

"That's really pretty Ri."

"Thank you."

"I like your mom and dad by the way. They are really cool."

"Thank you. They like you too."

"Did they tell you that?"

"No, but I can tell."

Mike smiled and said, "That's cool. So, how are you feeling?"

"I'm sore and exhausted, but I'm fine."

"I heard that you did a good job during delivery."

"Ha! I don't know who told you that. It took forever to push her out. I didn't think I was going to be able to. I can't even describe the feeling."

Mike chuckled and said, "Your mom told me that. Well, you survived, and look at this beautiful gift that you brought into this world. Congrats again."

"Thank you."

"Well, get comfortable, and I'm going to run your bath water and make you some lunch because I know you're hungry for some real food."

"Yes, I am for real. Hospital food is yuck."

Mike laughed and walked towards the bathroom. He turned on the water, and then walked to the kitchen to prepare lunch for Riley. Riley put her things away, and then she walked in the bathroom to enjoy a nice hot bath.

***

Riley was sitting on the couch at her mom and dad's house waiting for Jamir to show up. They were holding their grandchild and admiring how adorable she was. They were making all the sounds people make when they are talking to a baby. Riley loved to see how gushy they were over Raina.

"So, I've been wanting to ask you since the hospital, is your child's father married?" Riley's father asked.

Riley looked down at the ground and said, "Yes, dad he is."

"You had a baby by a married man, daughter?" Riley's mom asked.

She looked up and said, "Yes mom."

Her parents looked at each other, and then her dad asked, "Why are you looking like that?"

"Because I knew that this was going to come up."

"You didn't think that we were going to ask questions about the father of our grandchild?" her mother asked.

"No. I knew. I just didn't want to talk about it."

"We're just curious to know what happened because you told us that you two broke up. Now, we are finding out that he is married." her mother said.

Riley exhaled again and said, "I didn't know that he was married."

"So, basically he was cheating on his wife with you?" her dad asked.

"Yes." Riley said.

"Boy, boy, boy." her dad said.

"Does his wife or his family know about this baby?"

"She knows, but I don't think his family knows unless he told them."

Her father exhaled, "Boy, boy, boy." he repeated.

"You sure got yourself into a situation daughter." her mom said.

"I know."

"I don't like him. I didn't like him the moment he walked into the hospital room, so maybe it was good that you didn't end up marrying a guy like that. He's a coward. Cheating on his wife." her father said.

"Now, baby let's try not to judge. We don't know his situation. I don't like him either, but we're just trying to make some sense out of this situation. It sounds like you're going to be pretty much raising Raina by yourself, regardless if he chooses to be in the child's life or not, because of his marriage. Is that right?" her mom asked.

"Yes. I came to that reality while I was pregnant."

"Well, I hope that you learned your lesson." her father said.

"Daddy."

"I'm just saying baby. Nothing good comes from dealing with a married man." he said.

"I know, but he told me that he is going to be in our child's life as much as he can, so I'm going to give him the opportunity, but if he messes it up, then we will have to figure it out from there."

"Well, I guess that's all you can do right now." her mom said.

"Does he have kids with his wife?" her father asked.

"He has two. I believe one of them they just had right before me." Riley said.

"Boy, boy, boy." her father said.

Riley's mom exhaled and said, "Well, we'll just have to make lemonade out of lemons, so if you need anything, you know that you can call us. Ok?"

"Yes, mom. Thank you." Riley said.

"So, who was the guy that came to your party and to the hospital?" her mom asked.

"Mike? He's my neighbor."

"I like him." her mother said.

The doorbell rang. Riley's mom stood up to answer it.

Riley's dad rubbed his forehead and repeated, "Boy, boy, boy."

Jamir walked in and greeted her mom, and then he walked over to the couch and greeted her dad with a handshake. He leaned down to hug Riley and sat next to her on the couch. Riley handed him the baby.

"We're going to go back here to the family room and let y'all have some privacy." Riley's mom said.

"Ok." Riley said.

"Do you need anything before we go?" her mother asked.

"No." Riley said.

"Alright, well call us if you need us. It was good seeing you Jamir." her mother said.

"Thanks; likewise." Jamir said.

Riley's parents walked of the room. Jamir looked down at his daughter and smiled.

"She is gorgeous."

"Yea she is."

"She looks just like you."

"I don't know yet. Everyone says that she looks like you." Riley said.

"She definitely has my lips." Jamir said.

"She has your eyes too." Riley said.

"How have you been?"

"I've been good. Just settling into this new lifestyle."

"I hear you. You're looking good by the way."

"Thank you. What's been going on with you? Did your wife have her baby?"

"She did."

"Another boy?"

"Yea."

"Does she know about this baby?"

"She does. I finally came clean. We fought about it, but the reality is, she knew where I was, so it's not like it wasn't a possibility."

"Yea."

"Look Ri, I know I messed up. I know that you had feelings for me, and I should have been honest, but I was trying to have my cake and eat it too. I mean, me and my wife were going through some things, and I got on some whatever type stuff."

"It is what it is now. I'm just glad that you want to be here for Raina."

Jamir nodded his head. The two of them visited for a little while longer, and then he said he had to go. He told Riley that he had a bunch of things in the car for the baby. She asked her parents to watch the baby while she walked outside with him. His entire trunk was filled with bags of clothes and toys for the baby. She helped him put the bags into the trunk of her car. He gave her a hug, and then he left.

Chapter 15

Raelyn

Watching my sister give birth to my niece was one of the most beautiful experiences I've ever had, but it was also the most painful looking experience that I'd ever witnessed. It gave me mixed feelings about having children. After seeing that, I knew that I was in no rush to have children.

We were a few weeks into the new year, and I had finally talked to Aleyah. Besides the text that I had gotten from her New Year's Day, I hadn't seen nor talked to her. I needed find out why she was missing all that day. She said that she couldn't go into it, but she wanted to have a lady's night, so we could all get together to talk, and she could see the baby. After I got off the phone with her, I called my sister and set it up for the weekend. Riley said anytime worked for her because she was on maternity leave from work.

"I wish I could be there." Paris said.

"I know, but you have a trip already planned. To be honest, I wish that I was coming with you, so I can get out of this wintry weather for a while." I replied.

"If it wasn't such short notice, I would've brought you along."

"You're going for work anyway." I said, and then I took a sip of wine from my wine glass.

She did the same, and then she said, "So, you could've still tagged along. Well, maybe next time."

"Ok cool. I was thinking about planning a girl's trip for all of us."

"That would be cool. I've never been on one, but after seeing the movie, I've been wanting too."

"That movie was awesome by the way. Thanks for taking me." I said

"You're welcome. Well, let me know if you ladies decide to go because I would love to go."

"Ok cool. I will."

"On another note, did you ever talk to that dude again?"

"The one we went on a date with?"

"Yes him. The one we met at the club."

"That's right we've never talked about that. Girl no. He was so lame!" I said.

Paris busted into laughter.

I said, "I'm serious. Who cuts their buttermilk biscuit into pieces with a fork and knife? I was done."

Paris fell backwards onto the couch in a fit of laughter. She made me bust into a fit of laughter of my own.

"I'm serious." I said after I finished laughing.

Paris stopped laughing and said, "I understand."

"I need a real brotha. Not those high society bullshit kinds of guys. They are too far removed from the culture. There nothing wrong with an educated black man. I support that, but you can tell he hasn't been with a sista for a while. He probably thinks he can rub his fingers through my hair, and a true brotha knows that he can't do that."

Paris fell out laughing again.

I said, "Every brotha know the rules. You don't touch a black woman's hair unless you want to lose a hand or something."

"Oh, my goodness." Paris said.

"I'm just saying."

"My stomach hurts Rae. Girl you're too funny."

"I'm just being honest. Anyways. I know you like those kinds of guys, so are you still talking to the guy you met?"

"No. He looked good and he was everything I like, but his conversation was lame."

"Oh no."

"There is nothing worse than a man who doesn't have anything to talk about.

"They're the worst."

"Girl yes."

"He was a lame. We should go out again when I get back and see if we can meet some new guys."

"I'm going to pick the place this time where some real brotha's are at. It won't be ratchet."

"That will work, and hopefully we won't meet lames."

"For real." I said.

We clinked glasses, and then Paris said, "We are too beautiful for lames."

We swallowed down some wine, and then Paris leaned over and kissed me. She smiled flirtatiously. I had figured out by that time that alcohol made her frisky. It made me hot too, and that is why we had already hooked up a couple of times since the New Year. I didn't feel any kind of way about doing sexual things with her. It felt natural, and neither one of us were trying to be together. We were just having fun. Scratching each other's itch. Keeping each other company while we were both single and waiting for love to show up in the form of the right man.

I got up and straddled her, and then I said, "You want to see something?"

"What?" she giggled.

I giggled too. "It's just a little something, something." I said.

"Ok. Should I be scared?" she asked.

"No girl. Come on." I stood up and took her hand.

I helped her get up from the couch, and then I pulled her with me to my bedroom. She walked with me over to my cabinet and opened it. Her mouth dropped open when she saw my pleasure toy collection.

"Oh my Gawd Raelyn. I didn't know you had all this stuff in here. Girl, you're a freak!" she said.

I made an embarrassed facial expression and said, "No, I'm not."

"Yes, you are. I don't have any of this stuff. Not one."

"You can touch them. They're all clean."

Paris reached into the storage closet and pulled out one of the vibrators.

"This is cute. It looks like a lipstick."

"Yea girl I got that from the Kandy Koated collection."

"I've never seen anything like this before."

"I'll get you one." I laughed.

"No."

"Yes, every girl needs a vibrator."

I watched her look through my collection, and then I pulled out one of my favorites.

"Can I use this on you?"

"I don't know I'm scared." she giggled.

"Girl. It will be the best orgasm you've ever had in your life." I said.

She smiled and said, "Ok."

I told her to lay down. I climbed on top of her and kissed her for a while, and then I kissed her body down to her pearl. I gave her oral pleasure for a moment, and then I put the vibrating toy on her pearl. She closed her eyes and let me do my thing. Within in minutes, she was grabbing sheets and hollering my name.

When she came down from her orgasm, she said, "That shit is crazy Rae."

"I told you."

"I see why women be hooked on these."

"Girl, sometimes it's better than a man."

"Oh my God." she said as her body convulsed a few more times.

She sat up and crawled to me. We kissed for a while again, and then she told me to lay down. She used the same toy, but she sucked on my nipples while rubbing the toy on my pearl. In minutes, I was moaning curse words, and yelling that it felt good. After I stopped shivering, she turned the toy off and sat it on the bed next to her.

"This is my new best friend." she said.

I looked at her and started laughing. She climbed on top of me and put her pearl on mine, and then we kissed, rode each other, and rubbed pearls until we both busted together. When we were finished, we both passed out for a while, and then we got up and got dressed to go and meet Shawn.

Chapter 16

Shawn

I was walking out of the gym when I saw Raelyn and Paris walking through the doors of the community center. I met them at the door to greet them and welcome them to the community center.

"Hey ladies!" I said as I hugged them. "Welcome to the center. Come in."

"Hey Shawn! Thanks." Raelyn responded.

I noticed that she was glowing. She was smiling more than she'd been in a while. It was good to see her in a better mood.

"Paris, I know this is your first time here. Have you ever been to a community center?"

"I was in so many after school programs as a kid it was ridiculous." she replied.

I laughed and said, "Oh ok. Trust me, I understand. Well, the kids here are good kids. Misguided sometimes, but amazing and smart. They love Raelyn. They are going to love you too. Especially the boys because you're so beautiful."

"Awww, thank you." she said.

"You're welcome." I responded. "It's good to see you lady." I said to Raelyn.

"It's good to see you too Shawn." she smiled.

"You're looking beautiful and smiling more than usual."

"Thank you."

"You're welcome. I like that."

I hugged her again, and then I kissed her on the cheek. I turned to Paris and said, "I haven't seen her look so happy in a while. It must be you because I can't even make her smile like that."

Raelyn laughed and said, "Stop it Shawn."

Paris smiled and said, "Aww you two are cute."

Raelyn blushed and said, "Whatever Paris."

"Let me take you guys around to see the kids, and then we'll have lunch."

"Ok." the ladies responded.

I walked them around the center. We stopped in the gym first. The kids were excited to see Raelyn. A few of them ran up and hugged her. We stood in the gym and talked to the kids for a while, watched them play basketball, and then we walked over to the arts and crafts room. We walked around the room and looked at their art projects, and then we walked over to one of the rehearsal rooms. We watched a group of kids rehearsing dance routines for a show that they were invited to perform at.

"I wish I had all that energy." Paris said.

"Me too." I said.

"I wish that I could dance." Raelyn said.

Paris and I laughed, and then I said, "You can dance."

"Not like that. I can do a cute little two-step and a maybe a twerk here and there, but that's it."

"Yea, I feel you. I would probably break something if I did all that." Paris said as we turned to walk away.

I turned and looked at the entrance and saw the delivery guy walking through the door.

I said, "Our lunch is here. I ordered from your favorite place Rae. I got you what you like, and then I ordered a bunch of other stuff. I figured you would like something Paris. This place is amazing."

"Aww thank you." Raelyn said.

"That was thoughtful Shawn. Thanks." Paris said.

"Are you ladies ready to go and eat?"

"Yea." Raelyn said.

They followed me to the door. I paid the delivery guy, and then they followed me to a large conference room. I took the food out of the bag and put it on the table, and then I left and returned with paper plates, plastic silverware, and canned soda from one of the vending machines. We scooped food from the containers onto our plates and then we sat down to eat and chat.

"So, are you guys open every day?" Paris asked.

"Every day accept Sunday. It isn't as busy in here during the week. Saturday is our busiest day until summer. Once school is out kids are in here all the time; all week, and we have more programs going during the summer."

"Oh, that is really nice. I'm glad to see that we still have some stuff like this around."

"Barely. A lot of centers were closed because of funding, so we are blessed to still have ours. These kids need it. It keeps them out of trouble."

"I agree with that. It kept me out of trouble when I was young."

I heard the front door open, so I looked back, and saw my mom walking through the front doors.

"What? What is my mom doing here?" I asked as I stood up and walked towards the door of the conference room.

I walked out of the conference room and greeted my mom with a hug and a kiss on the cheek. Paris and Raelyn watched me chat with my mom through the glass windows. She said that she was out and about and had just dropped by to see me. I told her that I was having lunch with the ladies. She told me that she could leave, but I convinced her to stay and have lunch with us. I pointed towards the conference room, and then she followed me in there. I opened the door and let my mom walk in first, and then I followed her into the conference room.

"Ladies this is my mother Ms. James. Mom you remember Raelyn, and this is her friend Paris."

Paris said "Hi!" and then Raelyn said, "Hello Ms. James. It's good to see you again.

"Likewise, and you ladies can call me Lisa, Ms. James is too formal. I didn't mean to interrupt your lunch. I was just stopping by to visit my son since I was in the neighborhood."

"You're not interrupting. Please join us." Raelyn said.

"Yes please." Paris said.

"See I told you." I said.

My mother smiled. She walked over to an empty chair next to mine, sat down, and put her purse on the table. I picked up an empty paper plate and began putting food on it for my mom. I set the plate down in front of her, and then I left the room for a couple of minutes. I returned with a can of soda for her, and then I sat back down in my chair next to my mom.

"Thanks son and thank you ladies for letting me join your lunch." my mom said.

"Oh no problem at all. Thank you for joining us."

"You're welcome mom. We're glad you are here."

"This food is delicious. Where did you order it from?" she asked.

I said, "It's from Raelyn's favorite place. I surprised her and ordered it."

"Aww, that was really sweet of you son. I see that I taught you well." she said.

Raelyn smiled and said, "Yes you did."

"My son has always been a sweetheart. Even when he was little, he would always be doing things to put a smile on my face. I remember the first time he cooked me breakfast. He almost burned the house down, but he did a good job."

I laughed and said, "That's true."

"So, you're an only child?" Paris asked me.

"Yup." I replied.

"Yes. He almost had an older sister, but she passed away after I gave birth to her."

"Aww. I'm so sorry to hear that." Raelyn said.

"Oh, that is ok. I was devastated when it happened, but then I got pregnant and gave birth to this amazing man right here. I couldn't have asked for anything more. He has been a complete blessing to me."

"Awww that is beautiful Paris said."

"Thank you." she said.

I smiled, and then I kissed her on the cheek. "I love this woman right here. I would die for this woman."

Raelyn and Paris both said, "Awww. That is so sweet."

My mom said, "So Raelyn, I hear that you are a personal trainer."

"I am. I found my passion for health and fitness. I love looking and feeling good, and I enjoy helping others to do the same. I have to give credit to your son because he is the one that put the idea in my head and gave me the encouragement to take it on as a career."

"That's great Raelyn. That sounds like my son. Always spreading positivity. So, you're responsible for getting my son back into shape."

Raelyn laughed and said, "Yes he is, and partially. I give the tools and training, but it's up to the person to follow through. So, he has played a major part in getting himself back into shape as well."

My mom said, "I love it. Well, I might have to come and get some training from you."

"Absolutely, I would love that."

"Does she train you too?" she asked Paris.

"Yes ma'am. I wouldn't have it any other way. She is amazing."

"Awww. Thank you." Raelyn said.

"I told you Rae. I knew that you would be an amazing training, and she has built up a nice amount of clientele in just a short time." I said.

"Wow. Congratulations."

"Thank you."

"Yes. I'm so proud of her." I smiled at her.

Raelyn smiled back at me and took a bite of her food. "I'm proud of you too. You've really transformed your body."

"Yes, you have. I've noticed a change even in the brief time I've known you." Paris said.

"Well, thanks ladies." I said.

"I told you son. You got me wanting to get back into shape." my mom said.

"Y'all making a brotha feel really good right now. I appreciate the love." I smiled and took a bite of food.

We sat and chatted for a little while longer. My mom talked about some current news, church, and some kid that made her laugh on her flight back from visiting family in Iowa. Raelyn told us about her new baby niece, her parents church, her old job, and how we met. Paris told us about growing up in California and her life as a model. Once we were finished eating, they helped me clean up, and then my mom said that she had to leave.

"Well, I've got to get out of here. Thanks for letting me join you guys for lunch. It was great to talk to you ladies."

"You're welcome. It was great to talk to you too." Raelyn said.

"Yes, it was a pleasure." Paris said.

"I'll have to invite you two over for dinner sometime."

"Alright. We would love to come by."

"Ok. Well, son, I love you." my mom said. She reached out to hug me.

I embraced her and said, "I love you too mom."

She hugged Raelyn and Paris, and then she told them bye. We walked her to the door, and then Raelyn and Paris said that they needed to get out of there too. Raelyn said that she had clients that evening and needed to get home to prepare. I walked the ladies to their cars, and then I went back into the community center to finish my day.

Chapter 17

Raelyn

"That was really cool." Paris said as we got into my car.

"It really was. Shawn is cool." I said.

We put our seatbelts on, and then I put the key into the ignition, turned the car on, and pulled out.

"Shawn and his mom are really cool, but Shawn really loves you."

"What? Why do you say that?"

"What? You can't see the look in his eyes when he looks at you?"

"He doesn't look at me in any distinct way." I laughed.

Paris laughed and said, "Yes he does. It's this look of love and admiration. Like you could do no wrong. Girl that man is in love with you. Anyone can see that. Hell, a blind man could see that."

I laughed and said, "Shut up. Shawn is not thinking about me."

Paris laughed again and said, "You can be in denial all you want to. That man wants you."

"Whatever."

"It's not like he isn't a handsome guy. You two look good together. You would make a cute couple."

"I don't know. I just don't look at him like that. He's really not my type."

"Have you had sex with him?"

"Yes."

"Was it good?"

"Not the first time, but after that, it was."

"Girl you know the first time is weird most times. Because you're trying to feel each other out, but once you get comfortable, it goes down."

"Yea true. He did put it down after the first time. I was like damn, ok."

Paris laughed and said, "You should consider giving him a chance."

"Yea. My sister says the same thing. I don't know, but I will think about it."

"You should."

"Yea, well, anyways. This is the song right here."

I turned the radio up and let the music blast the rest of the ride back to my apartment. Paris and I sang all the songs together. When we made it back to my house, she jumped in her car and left, and then I headed to the gym to train a few of my clients.

Chapter 18

Aleyah

Aleyah was at Karina's house for a week. She was relieved when the police called to inform her that they had Niko in custody. They told her that they found him in her neighborhood about a block from her house a couple of days after she filed the report. Niko told them that he was driving through the neighborhood on his way somewhere, but to them, it looked like he was staking out the neighborhood looking for Aleyah and Lamar. He had circled the block many times, and one of their neighbors called about a suspicious car that kept driving around.

The neighbor told the police at one point, Niko had parked in front of their house and looked like he was just watching Aleyah and Lamar's home, and then he got out and started walking around the home peeping in windows. The neighbor told them that she didn't want any trouble, but the weird activity worried her. The police recognized Niko from Aleyah's report and searched his car. They said that they found more than one firearm in the car, and they had also found Aleyah's purse and phone in the car. They told Aleyah that she could pick her belongings up at the police station, and she agreed to press charges against Niko.

Aleyah walked out of her house with a couple of bags of luggage in her hands. She popped her trunk open and put the bags inside, she closed the trunk, and then walked to the driver's side of the car. After she got in, her phone started ringing.

"Hey Eazy." Aleyah said when she answered the phone.

"Sup. What you doing?" Eazy asked.

"Heading to meet up with Lamar."

"When do you got to do that?"

"In an hour."

"Ride down on me. I'm at the coffee shop on Lake street waiting on my boy. We about to meet and discuss some plans."

"Alright, but I can't stay long."

"I know. I just want to see you."

"Ok. I'm on my way."

Aleyah put the car in drive and headed to the coffee shop. It was cold outside that day and she had her heat blasting in the car. She turned it down once the car warmed up, and then she turned her radio up because she heard a song that she liked on the radio. Aleyah was in her thoughts the entire drive. Thinking about her decisions and what she could have done differently. She rode past a few people standing at bus stops and she thanked the creator that she had a vehicle. She took a left and drove past a couple of home owners shoveling snow from the sidewalk.

She made a mental note to tell Lamar that their walkway and sidewalk needed to be shoveled and some salt needed to be laid down. She had almost slipped on an ice patch going into the house. She pulled up to a stop light on Lake street. She sat there tapping her fingers on the steering wheel while watching and younger couple walk across the street. They were both wearing matching fur coats. Aleyah chuckled a little at how cute it was, and then she started driving when the light turned green. She found somewhere to park on the block, got out, paid to park at the meter, and then walked across the street to the coffee shop. The brisk air made her shiver the entire way.

She walked into the coffee shop rubbing her hands together to warm them up. Eazy stood up and waved his hand at her. She walked over to Eazy and gave him a hug.

"It is so cold out there."

"I know. I'll be glad when winter is over."

"Me too." Aleyah said as she sat down.

"How are you?" she said as she sat down.

"I'm good. Thanks for helping me Eazy. I really appreciate you for that." she said.

"No problem. You know that I will do anything for you. I'm just glad to see that you're ok. I see your bruise is gone." Eazy said.

"Yes finally. Now I don't have to cover it up with make-up."

"That's good. So, how are things going?"

"Um, well Niko was arrested, and I'll be going to court soon."

Eazy nodded his head and said, "I'm still shocked at the whole situation. I mean, I know what we did, but I've never known for you to cheat. I honestly thought that I was the only person you cheated with that one time. Not that it makes it right."

"There's more to it, but I don't have the time to go into it right now. At the end of the day, I did wrong and I'm paying for it."

"Does your husband know?"

"Yes. He knows everything now. Honestly, I feel worse now than I did when I was doing it. I mean, I was just having fun, but I didn't expect to almost lose my life over it."

"I hate to say it, but that's karma babe."

Aleyah exhaled and said, "I know."

"We all make mistakes. Don't beat yourself up over it. Just learn from it and move forward."

"Thanks. So, how are things with you?"

"The same. Putting together shows and dealing with Karina."

"Yea she's been talking my ear off about you this whole week."

"Yea? I bet it was a bunch of negative shit too, huh?"

"Nah. Not really."

He chuckled and said, "I don't even want to know. Anyways where are you heading?"

"To meet up with Lamar and have dinner. I guess he is ready to talk about everything. We haven't talked since the day it happened."

"Oh boy. Well, I hope that goes well."

"Me too. I got to get out of here though."

"Alright. It was good to see you. Hit me up and let me know how things go."

"I will."

They stood up, hugged, and then Aleyah left the coffee shop.

Chapter 19

Aleyah

It was Aleyah's first time seeing Lamar since the day it all went down. They felt that it was time to get together and address the situation since things had calmed down. He left little man at his cousin's house and hooked up for dinner. She was happy to see Lamar, but she also felt bad about the whole situation. she had already given herself a mental beat-down the week she was at Karina's. She knew that she should've been honest with Lamar about how unhappy she was in the marriage instead of stepping out on him.

"Hey." Lamar said when she met him outside of the restaurant.

"Hi." she responded.

"Are you ok?" he asked.

"Yes."

"Good. You look good."

"Thanks."

He hugged her and kissed her on the cheek. He was in a better mood than she expected him to be.

"Well let's go inside. It's cold out here." he said.

He opened the door to the Indian restaurant and followed her inside. The greeter seated them in a booth by the window and told them that a waiter would be over soon. They took their coats off and hung them on the coat hangers outside of the booth, and then they sat back down.

"I see the bruise is healing up." he said reaching across the table to touch her face.

"Yea. Finally."

"That's good." he said.

The waiter walked over to the table, introduced himself, and asked them if they wanted something to drink. They ordered waters and told the waiter to give them a couple of minutes to look at the menu. When the waiter walked away, the two of them looked through the menu in silence.

Aleyah found what she wanted, and then she put down the menu and said, "Lamar I'm sorry. I really, truly, apologize for what I've done. It was completely selfish, and I know that I broke a promise."

Lamar put his menu down and said, "I appreciate you apologizing again. I don't want you to think that I'm not mad because I am. I'm beyond pissed. I keep trying to figure out what you were thinking? Why you would do this to us? Why you would do this to our family?"

Aleyah's eyes filled with water. "I don't know. I was tripping. I just wanted to have some fun."

"By sleeping with another man? My best friend at that? I mean swinging wasn't enough? You just had to go and take it to another level?"

"I know." Aleyah said as she wiped tears.

"It's like. I thought about it so much. I can't even think about it anymore. The thought of it all makes my head hurt. I'm just happy that he did not hurt you like he could have. He could have taken you out of this life and away from our son. I don't care what me and you are going through, I couldn't think of our son living through life without his mom over some dumb shit, so I thank God that he spared your life and let you get away that day. I don't know how I would have felt, or how I would have explained it to our son, if the police would have shown up at our door to tell me that you were dead."

Aleyah nodded her head and wiped more tears. Lamar handed her some napkins. She dabbed her tears, and then the waiter returned to take their orders. They ordered their food and handed the waiter their menus.

When the waiter left, Aleyah said, "I fucked up."

"You're damn right you did, but I have to take responsibility for my part in this. I invited him into our bedroom. I opened the door, so I fucked up too." Lamar shook his head, and then he asked, "Do you know how much I love you?"

"I do."

"No really; do you?"

"I do Lamar."

"I don't think you do. I love you so much that I let you talk me into swinging just to make you happy. Once we did it, it was fun, and I liked it, but I could have done without it. It's not stuff that I do. I was just trying to make you happy."

"I understand."

"Maybe that's where we went wrong. We weren't being honest with each other. When we moved back, I really wasn't trying to live that life anymore. We did a lot of hanging out and partying while we were in Atlanta, and I was ready to put it all behind us and settle down, but instead of telling you, I just fell back. I figured you would notice and fall back with me. I don't know why I thought that because I knew you were bored. You've always been bored in our relationship, so you went out searching for fun. I understand, but it shouldn't be like that."

"You're right."

"We were young when new got together, and we barely knew each other when you got pregnant, or when we got married, but we've worked through most of it. Sometimes people grow apart and maybe we have."

"I agree."

"Not being honest with each other, shouldn't have made you do what you did though. That decision could have cost you your life, and possibly mine and our son's depending on where Niko was mentally."

They stopped talking briefly, so the waiter could put the food they ordered on their table. They both put their napkin in their laps, said grace, and began eating.

Aleyah said, "I was trying to end it with him Lamar, but he wasn't trying to let me go. I wasn't intending for all this to happen when I made the decision to do it."

"Do you think anybody is, when they're on bullshit? Do you remember what happened to that girl we went to high school with?" Lamar asked.

"Briana?"

"Yea. Do you think that she was intending for that to happen in her situation?

"I'm sure that she didn't."

"I mean come on. We're grown, but the moral of the story is, you fucked up and so did I, so I think that we should get legally separated, but work on fixing things, and if we can't fix them, we should consider going our separate ways. I keep thinking about our child and how all this will affect him, and I'm saying that I'm willing to work on it if you are, but I think that some time apart would be better for us because I need some time to get over this. Do you want to do that?"

Aleyah finished chewing another bite of food, swallowed and said, "Yes, I do. I've already found a place, and I've been slowly moving some of my stuff into it."

"I noticed. I've been by the house. That was quick. I actually thought that you were staying with Karina." Lamar said before taking a bite of food, and then washing it down with a few gulps of water.

"I was, and I love my best friend, but I need my own space." Aleyah said.

"I understand."

"Karina knows a lady who owns an apartment building and she had an apartment available right away, so Karina hooked it up. I went to look at the place, and it was nice, so she said I could move in right away. She didn't even make me fill out an application or do a background check."

"That's cool, well, as long as you and our son will be comfortable and safe there."

"We will."

"I know that you have to go to court, so I will come with you."

"Thank you."

"I want to see Niko anyways. I want to see the man that calls himself my brother, but then sleeps with my wife repeatedly behind my back and tries to abduct her. That's some shit. He better pray that I don't try to whoop his ass in the courtroom."

"Don't do that Lamar. I don't need you in jail too."

"You're right."

"Thank you for dinner."

"No problem. I'll help you move what you need to your new spot."

"Ok. Thank you for having this talk with me."

"It was needed. We will take it one day at a time."

They finished their dinner, left the restaurant, and went their separate ways.

Chapter 20

Riley

"She is so adorable." Aleyah said.

She looked down at Riley's baby girl that she had cradled in her arms. The baby was asleep but Aleyah couldn't get enough at how angelic she looked. Raelyn, Taji, and Cherry agreed that Riley's little angel was a bundle of cuteness.

Riley smiled and said, "Thank you."

"How has it been being a new mom?" Aleyah asked.

"It has been good. She's been pretty much sleeping unless she's hungry."

"Awww that's good. No sign of the baby daddy yet?"

A symphony of lip smacking, teeth sucking, and grunts went around the room.

"Huh? What did I miss?" Aleyah asked.

"Girl. He showed up at the hospital unexpected." Riley said.

"No way." Aleyah said.

"Yup, and I was ready to smack the shit out of him." Raelyn said angrily.

"We all were." Taji said while scratching her bulging belly.

"I guess he felt bad for denying her, so he showed up at the hospital." Riley said.

"Wow." Aleyah said.

"Girl, but he's been around to see her since. I've had him meet me at my parent's house to visit her. I'm not

ready for him to be at my house again, so I feel my parents'
house is safe."

"I understand."

"Mom and dad can't stand him." Raelyn said.

"I know. Especially dad." Riley said.

"You should have seen my dad's face at the hospital
when he realized who Jamir was. He looked like he wanted
to kill him." Raelyn said to Aleyah.

Aleyah chuckled and said, "I wish I was there to see
that. I apologize that I didn't make it.

"Speaking of that, why weren't you there? Your
husband was calling around looking for you."

"Well, a lot has happened. That is why I wanted to
get together." Aleyah said.

She stood up, walked over to Taji, and handed the
baby to her. She adjusted her pants and sat back down.

"What I'm about to tell you guys can't leave this
house." Aleyah said.

"Oh boy." Raelyn said.

Aleyah laughed and said, "You're right. Lamar and I are separated."

Riley gasped, and then the entire room fell silent.

"I've moved out. Our son is with me."

"Shut up." Riley said.

"Are you serious?" Raelyn asked.

"Um hum." Aleyah said.

"I'm sorry girl." Cherry said.

"It's ok. It's my fault." Aleyah said.

"What happened?" Riley asked.

"Well, I was having an affair, and I didn't make it to the hospital because the guy I was having an affair with kidnapped me."

"What!?" Raelyn asked.

"When!?" Cherry asked.

"New Year's Eve night. After I left the club."

"Who!?" Riley asked.

"Niko." Aleyah said.

"Fine ass Niko?" Riley asked.

"Yup." Aleyah said.

"I told y'all that he was crazy." Taji said.

"You know Niko?" Aleyah asked Taji.

"Yes girl, and I wish that I didn't. I used to mess with him on the side, and then he started stalking me. I told the twins about it."

"Yes sis. I was going to tell you about it because I was worried that something was going on between you two, but I didn't see or talk to you until New Years, and then the whole situation happened at the party with my brother and Karina."

"I remember getting a text message from you telling me to call you, but I was busy with holiday stuff. It's ok now. He's in jail."

"Thank God." Taji said.

"Who does that kind of crazy shit nowadays?" Riley asked as she stood up. She walked over to get the baby from Taji, so she could start feeding her.

"Apparently crazy ass mofo's like him. He knocked me out and ran off with me to Chicago. He was on the way to Virginia."

"Virginia?!" Raelyn asked.

Taji said, "That is where he is from. Most of his family is there. He moved to Chicago with his dad when he was young, and he went back and forth from Chicago to Virginia most of his life until he moved up here to Minnesota."

"So, he was going to take you all the way to Virginia?" Raelyn asked.

"That's what he said. That was his plan. To hold me hostage there and marry me. By the grace of God, I got away. I don't even know how I managed to get away."

"You have got to be kidding me." Riley said.

"Seriously." Aleyah said.

"Wow." Cherry said.

"I'm glad that you are ok." Riley said.

Aleyah replied, "Thank you."

"I knew there was something going on with you and him sister, but why though?" Raelyn asked.

Aleyah said, "It's a lot."

"Enough to cheat?" Raelyn asked.

"The truth is… Lamar and I have been swingers for years. We swung with Niko, and then me and Niko took it further." Aleyah said.

Raelyn's eyebrows went up.

"Wow." Riley said.

"Damn girl y'all some freaks." Cherry said.

"I could never do it. That is right up Raelyn's lane." Riley said.

"Shut up. I was never a swinger."

"Yea, but you were a relationship with a couple."

"Whatever." Raelyn said to her sister, and then she looked at Aleyah and said, "I'm actually shocked right now."

"So, y'all were having sex with other couples?" Cherry asked.

"Yes, we were." Aleyah said.

"Wow." Raelyn said.

"Damn y'all some straight up freaks. I've never done anything like that. I think that's beyond Raelyn." Taji said.

"Shut up." Raelyn laughed.

"I don't mean to pry, but did y'all use condoms with him?" Taji asked.

"Yea."

"Ok good."

"Why?"

"Well, I don't know if this is true, but there was a rumor that Niko has the package." Taji said.

"What?"

"Yea, I don't know, but I got checked, and y'all might want to as well just to be on the safe side." Taji said.

"Oh my God." Aleyah said.

"I know. I hate to bearer of bad news. I got checked and nothing, but it's better to know than not know." Taji said.

"That's true. Ugh. Now I have to tell Lamar that on top of telling him that I'm pregnant?"

"You're pregnant girl?" Raelyn asked.

"Yes. I just found out, and Lamar doesn't know yet. We really haven't been talking, but we start these therapy sessions tomorrow. He wants to work on the marriage."

"Congrats girl." Riley asked.

"Thanks. It was a total surprise, and it is Lamar's baby if you heifers were questioning."

The ladies started laughing. "I'm not going to lie. I was." Cherry said.

"I was too." Riley said.

"Whatever y'all." Aleyah said.

"I'm just saying." Raelyn said.

"Make sure you and your husband go and get checked for real. Especially for your baby."

"You're right. We will."

*****

Riley looked at Jamir sitting next to her on her parent's couch holding their daughter Raina. She silently wished that they had the family life together, but it wasn't like that. He had his family with Kiesha and Riley was on the outside with his child. Riley wondered if she wasn't so gone over him, would she had allowed the pregnancy to happen. She questioned if she would've even continued to see him, after she found out that he was still married. Riley realized in that moment that had been so stuck in a fairytale world that she was blind to reality the entire time that she was dealing with Jamir. She wished she could go back and take it all back, but it was too late, their daughter was born, and Riley had no choice, but to work with her situation the way it was.

"Are you ok out here?" Riley's mom asked.

Jamir and Riley looked up and saw her standing in the doorway leading to the back area of the house. The light from the hallway was shining behind her. She was wearing a sundress, and a pair of slippers on her feet.

"Yes, we are." Riley replied.

"Ok. Let me know if you need anything." her mom said, and then she turned and walked to the back of the house where Riley's father was.

Jamir looked back down at his daughter and Riley focused her eyes back on Jamir.

"She has so much hair." he said.

"I know."

"You're going to have fun dealing with that."

"I got my stylist on deck when that time comes." Riley said.

Jamir laughed, and then he said, "I think that she has your fingers and toes."

Riley laughed and said, "I noticed that, but she looks like you though."

"Yea you keep saying that. That's what my uncle says."

"You told your family about her?"

"My uncle is the only person that knows so far. He said I wouldn't be able to deny her even if I tried."

Riley thought about how he denied the baby during the pregnancy and said, "You did try."

Jamir sighed and said, "I know. I'm sorry Riley. I was on some fuck boy shit. I didn't want to admit it to Kiesha because she was already tripping."

"So, you tried to make me look stupid, and then you disrespected me in the process."

"It wasn't like that. I was just trying to run away from it. I didn't want to give Kiesha something else to be fussing about. Especially when we were trying to fix our marriage."

"Why were you still messing with me, if you were trying to fix your marriage?"

"I like you Riley. You're a good woman. I just couldn't give you what you wanted."

"I wish you would've been honest from the start. I was in love with you. I didn't want this to be like this. I wanted us to be a family."

"I know, and I'm sorry that I can't give you that."

"Thanks for apologizing. As long as you're here for her. That's all that matters."

"I'm going to be here for my baby. I promise you that. Speaking of that, I know that you're not comfortable with me coming around yet, and that is understandable, but how long will we have to meet at your parents? I'm just saying, when can I come to your place and see my daughter?"

"I don't know about that yet."

"I'm just saying. It's uncomfortable being over here. Your dad is always snarling at me when he sees me."

Riley laughed and said, "He does not snarl."

"Humph. Close to it."

"I know that I did some fuck boy shit, but damn a brotha ain't perfect."

Riley laughed and stood up, so she could take the baby from him and put her into her car seat. She didn't know why Jamir thought he deserved to be accommodated to make him feel comfortable, after what he'd put her through, but she understood. Riley knew that her parents hated him, and they were cordial, but they weren't nice to him. She could feel the negative energy every time he walked in the door.

"I'll think about it." Riley said.

Riley started packing everything up, so they could leave. He stood up, hugged her, and then he kissed the baby. Riley called for her parents to tell them that they were leaving. They said bye to her parents, and then Jamir walked her to the car and helped her strap the baby in. After Jamir helped her with the baby, he hugged her again, and then he walked to his car.

Chapter 21

Eazy

Karina took our daughters hand and rolled her eyes at me. I looked up at the sky and shook my head.

"Why do you always have an attitude when you see me?" I asked.

"Because you get on my nerves." she said.

"What did I do now?"

"I bet you had her around your little girlfriend again huh?"

"Here you go. That's not your business."

"It is when it comes to my daughter."

"Your back to this bullshit again. We just talked about this."

"Whatever."

I shook my head and said, "I'm not with that girl anymore."

She twisted her lips and said, "Yea right."

"I'm not, and it's your fault. I'm sure that makes you happy, so you can just stop with the attitude."

"Whatever."

"Yea. I bet."

"Anyways. Did you remember Princess's backpack?"

"Shit I forgot." I said.

"See you're always forgetting stuff, and you wonder why I have an attitude."

"Don't use this as an excuse. It's not that serious."

"It is."

"I'll bring it by here tomorrow."

"She needs it tomorrow morning."

"Damn."

"I'll just stop by to pick it up tonight on my way home from Sunday dinner at my mom's."

"I got things to do tonight. I don't have time to be waiting on you."

"What? Another bitch?"

"Karina." I said, and then she rolled her eyes again.

"I got a club event tonight."

"Well, I'm not going to be waiting on you in the morning when I got to go to work, so I'll be by tonight. I'll text you when I'm on my way from my mom's house."

"Don't have me waiting, or I'm going to leave, and then bring it to you in the morning."

"Tell my Princess to come here, so I can give her a kiss."

"Princess come and say goodbye to your daddy." Karina called into the house.

Our daughter ran back to the door and jumped into my arms.

"Bye daddy." she said.

"Bye Princess." I said.

I kissed her on her cheek, and then I put her back onto her feet. She stood next to her mom and watched me walk to my car and get in. They waved when I started my car, and then Karina closed the door. I pulled off to go and handle some business.

***

I was rushing through my house trying to finish getting dressed so I could get to my event on time. I stopped in my bedroom mirror, so I could check how I looked. I started buttoning up my shirt. I was feeling my outfit for the night. I was wearing all designer labels, and my jewelry was shining. People would say that I was dripping in ice, and I would say that my neck and wrist were frozen. I finished buttoning up my shirt, and then turned to the side to peep my whole profile. The extra time that I had been putting in the gym was paying off.

My arms were huge, and you could see them bulging through my shirt. I could see why people said that I was my dad's twin. I turned back to face the mirror, picked my hair brush up off my dresser, and brushed my hair. My three-sixty waves were popping just like I liked them. I heard my doorbell, so I put my brush into my back pocket and walked down the stairs. I knew that it was Karina stopping by to get our daughters backpack. When I got to the door, I opened it and walked away.

"The bag is in her room." I said as I walked to my hall closet to find shoes to wear.

"Dang you're not even going to speak to me?" she asked.

"I just did." I called across the room.

She closed the front door and said, "Yea to tell me where her bag is. You didn't say hi."

"Karina don't start." I said.

She walked inside my house, closed the door, and walked to our daughter's bedroom. She came out with our daughter's bag in hand. I could hear the heels of her boots clicking against my hardwood floors as she walked towards me.

"You look good." she said.

"Thanks." I said without looking up.

"Where's our daughter?" I asked.

"My roommate Shalita took her home after dinner."

"Oh aight."

She sat down on my steps and asked, "So, what concert is this? The Cardi B concert?"

"Yup and we are sold out too. I'm sure it's going to be hella lit tonight." I replied.

I found the shoes that I was looking for, but I also found another pair that I liked just as much, so I pulled them both out of the closet. I put one shoe on my left foot and then I put the opposite shoe on the right foot.

I turned towards her and asked, "Which one?"

She gave me a slight smile, looked me up and down, and then she pointed to the shoe on the left foot.

"That one." she said.

"Alright cool. That's the shoe that I picked originally."

"What girl are you taking with you to the concert tonight?" she asked.

I chuckled, "See. Here you go. Nobody, nosey ass."

She giggled and shook her head.

I said, "What? You're about as nosey as my sisters."

"Whatever."

"Don't start no shit. I ain't with it tonight."

"I'm not."

"Aight."

"Here let me help you." she said.

She stood up and walked over to me. She started adjusting the collar of my shirt. I wasn't aware that it was looking crazy. I didn't know how I missed that when I was standing in the mirror.

"Thanks." I said while she was fixing it.

"No problem." she said, and then she kissed me.

I asked, "Why did you do that shit?"

I wiped her lip gloss off my lips and backed away from her.

"I just miss you."

"Yea, well, you ain't got to be kissing me and shit." I said as I bent down to change the non-matching shoe.

She smacked her lips and said, "I miss us Eazy."

"Arguing?"

"No, the fun times. I think we should get back together. We should be together for Princess."

"You already know that's not going to happen."

"Why?"

"Because we don't get along. All we do is fight. We'll be straight for a little while, and then we will be back to the same old shit."

"Things might've changed."

"Since when? Up until a couple of months ago, you were about that drama. The only reason you've been chill is because I went off on you. You'll be back tripping in no time."

"Maybe I'm ready to do right."

"Tell that to someone who doesn't know you. We've already been down this road and it didn't work."

"Yea, but we were both dating other people. It wasn't a fair chance."

"Yea because we were dating to see if we could get along long enough to take it further and what happened?"

She rolled her eyes and folded her arms.

I said, "Right. You came to the club drunk and tripping, and then we got into a huge argument at the club. I almost got arrested that night fucking with you."

"Because you were all in that chick's face, dancing with her, and knowing that I was there the entire time."

"We weren't together Karina. We were dating."

"So, that was disrespectful."

"How?"

"You were doing it in my face."

"Like I haven't seen you flirting and giving other dudes your number in my face. Come on now."

"That's neither here nor there."

"Why ain't it? You can do the shit, but I can't? Get out of here."

"That's not what I'm saying."

"Look, I'm not about to argue with you about this. What's done is done. I've got to get out of here. I'm running late."

She stood there with her arms still folded while staring at me with a straight face.

"Eazy."

"What?"

"I love you."

"Ok whatever. You need to work on your attitude and decision making." I said.

I walked over to my coffee table. I picked up my key and wallet, and then I walked to my door. I opened the door and waited for her to follow me. She walked towards me with her arms still folded. When she got to me, she kissed me again.

I said, "Quit that shit."

I wiped her lip gloss off my lips again. She nudged my head backwards with her fingertips and said, "Whatever."

"See there you go with that attitude. Check that shit."

"Whatever." Karina called back as she walked towards her car.

"You know damn well there ain't no better woman than me, so you should just stop trying because you're not going to find her." she said before getting into her car.

She slammed her car door, put her car into drive and pulled out. I shook my head, locked the door to my house, and walked to my car. I remembered when I used to try to fuck her attitude out of her. That didn't do anything but make it worse. There was no chance of us ever getting back together ever again. I wasn't going to put myself through that drama again. I put my car into drive and headed to the club.

Nia Rich

Chapter 22

Karina

Karina walked into the house, took her shoes off and walked into the living room. Princess ran out of her room and wrapped her arms around her mom's legs. Karina bent down to hug her, and then she walked over to the couch and sat down next to Shalita.

"That took forever. I thought you were just going over there to pick up her bag?"

"I did."

"What took you so long then?"

"We were talking."

"About what?"

"About the concert tonight and Princess."

"That must have been a pretty lengthy conversation. You've been gone for over an hour."

"No, it wasn't." Karina said.

Shalita gave Karina a side eye, and then she said, "Let me find out that you're still trying to get back with him."

Karina made a screwed up facial expression and said, "I'm not."

"Don't lie to me Karina." Shalita said.

"I'm not. I'm about to give Princess her bath and get her ready for bed." Karina said as she stood up and walked to Princess's room.

Shalita watched her walk away. She had her suspicions about Karina and Eazy's relationship, but she didn't press. Shalita picked up the remote control and began channel surfing while Karina was in the bathroom with Princess.

***

"You like that?" Shalita asked.

"Yes, I do." Karina moaned.

Shalita thrusted in and out of her a little harder. Karina kept her legs spread open while Shalita went to work on her with her plastic black strap on. She'd found the perfect rhythm and was just waiting for Karina to let her know that she was going to have an orgasm. She loved to watch Karina cream all over the detachable tool. Karina knew that she had her there when Karina started thrusting back.

"Ah yea. Right there. Don't stop baby." Karina whined.

Shalita continued to thrust with her attachment in and out of Karina until Karina cried out that she had reached her peak. Shalita smiled and watched Karina cream on the toy.

"Ah yes!" Karina cried out as she shook and shivered.

Shalita thrusted a little slower until Karina was done getting hers. After Karina stopped shaking, Shalita pulled the toy out of Karina, took the attachment off, and laid next to Karina. Karina turned over, curled up next to her, and kissed her.

"Damn baby that was good. I love you." Karina said.

"Um hum. I love you too."

"What does um hum mean?"

"Because you be lying to me. You took forever tonight and I'm trying to figure out why?"

"Baby. You're thinking way too far into it. I just went over there to get the bag, chatted with him for a minute and came home."

"And that's it?"

"That's it. I swear."

"Ok." Shalita said.

"So, have you thought about what we talked about? Telling people about us?" Shalita asked.

"Baby I told you. That is going to take time."

"That was a while ago, and I know you seen how your mom was looking at us today. People are already speculating."

"No, they're not."

"Yes, they are."

"All they know is you're my friend and roommate, and that is all they need to know."

"They need to know that I'm your woman. I'm tired of being in the background. Especially when I think you're still trying to get back with your baby daddy, or he is trying to get back with you."

"Girl please. Don't nobody want his ass ok."

"That's what you say, but I don't think you're being truthful."

"Baby. I'm done with him. Been done. I love you, so stop being insecure."

"Insecure?"

"Yes. You're too worried about everyone else."

"I'm not insecure. I just want my woman to be truthful with me and acknowledge me."

"I am being truthful, and I do acknowledge you."

"Yea in the dark."

Karina climbed on top of Shalita and started kissing her.

"Don't try to shut me up by kissing me." Shalita said.

Karina kept kissing her until she kissed her back, and then Karina kissed her down her body until she reached her love button. She sucked and licked Shalita out of her questions and concerns, and into making sounds pleasure with her head tilted to the ceiling. Karina licked and sucked Shalita into another place where no worries about who knew about them existed. Shalita grabbed Karina's head and squealed when she reached her peak.

"Ah baby, yes, right there." she cried out.

She froze and tried to push Karina's head back, but Karina kept going until Shalita was begging her to stop.

"Baby please stop." Shalita begged.

"Are you sure?"

"Yes, baby please."

Karina smiled and said, "Ok."

She started kissing Shalita's body back up to her lips. She tongue kissed Shalita a little, sharing the flavor of her juices, and then she laid next to her.

"Damn baby you do that shit so good." Shalita whispered.

"I know. That's why you love me."

"I do love you. I just want to be in the open."

"We will be soon babe."

"Ok."

Chapter 23

Aleyah

Aleyah and Lamar were sitting across from each other in the court building cafeteria having lunch. It had been a few months since they separated and started living in separate households. It was Aleyah's first time living alone since her brief stint in college before getting pregnant. The time alone was refreshing, but there were many nights that she missed Lamar and wished that she wasn't sleeping alone; especially while pregnant with their second child.

The two of them weren't talking much. They had both been picking up little man from school on opposite days, and they very seldomly communicated over the phone. The only time Aleyah saw Lamar was at the therapy sessions. She told him that she was pregnant during one of those sessions. They talked briefly about the pregnancy after the session, but that was it. The court hearing, they were at was their first time having an in-depth conversation since they did at dinner a while back.

"I can't believe that he had the nerve to plead not guilty and say that I went with him willingly." Aleyah said.

"I know. I was taken aback by that. His punk ass wouldn't even look at me the whole time we were in that court room. He knows he ain't shit. I kept having to tell myself not to jump over the banister and put hands on that muthafucka." Lamar said.

Aleyah said, "Uuuuggh, I'm so mad. Mostly mad at myself because I knew better. I just didn't think that it would turn out like this."

Lamar put his plastic cup of soda back on the table and said, "Yea. You messed up. Real bad Aleyah."

"I know." she said. Water filled up her eyes.

"Don't start that crying."

"I'm sorry. I just wish that I could take it all back. Even the swinging days. Just all of it." Aleyah said, and then she caught her tears with her finger before they could fall onto her face and mess up her make-up.

Lamar handed her one of the napkins from off the table, and then he said, "It's too late to take it back now."

"Thank God our HIV tests came back negative." Aleyah said.

"I know. We should get tested again in a few months just to be on the safe side. I mean honestly, I heard the rumor years ago, but I knew that it wasn't true. Someone was trying to slander his name for some stuff he did back then. I would have never agreed to inviting him into our bedroom, if I felt that it was true."

"I know. It was scary hearing that. Especially from someone he used to mess with. You never know these days. You think for sure he is safe because he is our close friend, and then you hear something different. It had me shook for a while. It made me question the other people we had swung with too. I'm just glad that we used protection."

"I know. Me too. I've certainly learned my lesson. I hope you have too."

"I have. I'm sorry that I put our family through this. I'm still shocked at how crazy Niko really is." Aleyah said while shaking her head.

Lamar said, "I wish you would've talked to me about him. I could have told you. I knew that he was a little off. I've always known since we were kids, but it was never anything to be alarmed about. He had some minor problems from childhood trauma. The bi thing is true. I've always known that. Some shit happened to him as a kid that made him like that. He never tried me, so it never bothered me."

"Wow." Aleyah said before taking a sip from her cup of soda.

"Yea he went through a lot as a kid. I knew he struggled with depression. He really lost it when his wife died. He married young like us. Faye was there with him through all of it. She kept him sane and on his medication. They've always been tight since their Chicago days. He met her in Chicago where he met and married his wife. He followed Faye up here to Minnesota after his wife passed. They love each other, but they've always had an open relationship." Lamar said.

"He told me he killed his wife. Is that true?"

"Nah., she got hit with a stray bullet at a night club they were at. She died in his arms. He was never the same after that. He went into a deep depression. When he came out of it, he started partying, smoking, and drinking a lot. It was his way of coping. Then, he got locked up. As far as I knew, he got locked up for trying to retaliate against the dudes that killed his wife. This stalking and kidnapping stuff is new to me."

"Wow. That's really messed up."

"It is man, and that is why I have mixed emotions about this whole thing, because I know his story, but at the same time, he did me dirty, and I just want to fuck him up one more time."

"I understand. It's all my fault."

"Nah it's not just you. Like I told you, I take fault in this too, because I invited him in. I gave you the green light. I'm just as much to blame as you. That's why I suggested counseling, so we can try to fix this, and move forward. I never wanted our son to be raised in separate households, and now you're about to have another child. We gotta try to make things right."

Aleyah nodded her head and asked, "Did you tell your family what's going on?"

"Not in details. I just told them that we were working through some things."

"Same here."

"They said they were praying for us." Lamar said.

Aleyah nodded her head again and said, "My family said the same thing."

"I'm going to stand by your side through this court bullshit. That muthafucka is going to pay. He is either going to do the time, or he's going to answer to me in these streets. I'm a church boy, but I don't play when it comes to my family or my life."

Aleyah sat silent for a few minutes as flash backs of sitting in the car with Niko ran through her mind. She took a few more bites of her food and watched a few people walk into the cafeteria and order food.

"I can't believe he kidnapped me." she said after being silent for a while.

"I can't believe it either. This is shit that happens in the movies. Not real life."

Lamar looked at his watch and said, "We gotta go back to the court room."

Aleyah said, "Ok."

They stood up, packed up their food, walked over to put it into the trash, and then headed back up to the courtroom.

Chapter 24

Raelyn

"Ok. I got one." I said.

I made a serious facial expression, changed my vocal tone, and said, "You told Harpo to beat me?"

Paris and Shawn busted into laughter.

Paris said, "The Color Purple! That was an easy one."

Shawn said, "Yea, Rae that was too easy."

Paris said, "Ok. I got one."

She frowned and said, "What the fuck you stealing boxes for? You tryna build a clubhouse?"

The three of us busted into laughter again.

Shawn said, "Friday! That was easy too!"

"Yea it was!" Raelyn said.

"Shawn it's your turn." I said as I poured us more shots.

"Ok. I got y'all after this shot." Shawn said.

The three of us clinked shot glasses, and then we swallowed down the shot.

Shawn wiped his mouth and said, "Look Kiesh! I don't know no fucking Kiana's!"

Paris and I yelled, "Belly!"

The three of us laughed, and then Shawn growled and barked like the rapper that played the part in the movie.

We laughed some more, and then Shawn said, "For real though Rae. Congrats on getting a celebrity client."

"Thank you! I cannot believe it. I never imagined getting a celebrity client when I started my business."

"Yes, girl I am so happy for you!" Paris said.

"Thank you."

"You are so dope! Isn't she so dope?" Paris asked Shawn.

"Yes, she is. That's why I love her so much. She knows that I love her, but she just won't give me a chance. Tell your friend to give me a chance."

"You heard the man. He's a good guy. Give him a chance." Paris said.

I started laughing as I poured us more shots. Shawn held up his shot glass and said, "To more success, and to Raelyn giving a brotha a chance."

We laughed, clinked glasses, and then swallowed down the shot. All three of us were tipsy and close to our alcohol limits. After we set our shot glasses on the counter, Paris hugged me from behind, and then she started placing kisses on my neck. I smiled and looked at Shawn. His eyebrows went up, but he didn't take his eyes off us. I turned around and started tongue kissing her.

"Wooow. Ok." we heard Shawn say from behind us while we were kissing.

We started giggling, and then we stopped kissing.

We turned to face him, and then I giggled again and said, "Sorry."

"No need. I'm just saying. I didn't know it was like that."

Paris giggled and said, "Sorry Shawn. She's such a good kisser. I'm sure you already know that."

I smiled and said, "He does."

I walked over to him and kissed him. Paris watched us kiss with a smile on her face, and then she walked over and joined us in the kiss. Shawn fell into the moment and started kissing both of us. He tasted my lips, he tasted hers, and then he stopped.

"Hold up. What are y'all trying to do?"

I smiled and said, "Come on."

"Are y'all serious?" he asked

Paris laughed and said, "Yes."

Paris took his hand in hers. I took his other hand, and then we turned, and started walking towards my bedroom. Shawn allowed us to pull him in there. We didn't bother to turn on the lights. We started kissing him and taking his clothes off. Once we got his shirt off, we began kissing his neck and chest, and then we started unbuckling his pants. Paris pulled his pants down and kneeled in front of him. She took his manhood out, kissed it, and then put it into her mouth. I started kissing him again while she went to work on him, and then I kneeled and joined her.

We kissed, licked and sucked on his manhood, and then we switched it up and took turns. One on the jewels and one on the tool. When I looked up at him, he looked like he was in double pleasure heaven. Paris and I hadn't lost our touch since the Laron days.

We stopped giving him pleasure long enough to stand up, get undressed, and pull him to the bed. After he laid down, we went back to giving him double oral pleasure. He made loud sounds the entire time we were devouring him. After a while, I stopped, crawled up to his face, and sat my peach on his tongue. Paris continued feasting on his tool while I fed him my peach. Sounds of Shawn and I moaning and Paris slurping on his manhood was all you could hear in my room. Paris stopped tasting him, straddled him, and put him inside her. He moaned when he felt her, and then he grabbed her backside and thrusted up into her. She started making sounds that matched mine. She grinded on his manhood while I grinded on his face. We hadn't been in that position since we were with Laron. He crossed my mind for split second, and then I shook the thought. My orgasm took over. It made me freeze, and then I moaned Shawn's name.

"Mmmm Shawn." I said.

"Eat her pussy Shawn." Paris said, and then she smacked my backside.

"Ah Fuck!" I squealed with my head towards the ceiling. I dropped my head down and grabbed the headboard as my orgasm shook my body.

Shawn was doing well handling two women his first time. I climbed off him, and then he told Paris to get up. He grabbed my leg and pulled me to the edge of the bed. Paris crawled over and sucked her juices off his manhood, and then she watched him enter me. She put her peach on my face while facing him, and then she held my legs open as he pounded into me. Paris told him to kiss her.

"Kiss me." she moaned.

Shawn leaned forward and started kissing her. The feeling of my tongue on her pearl got to her and she started bouncing on my face. She stopped kissing him and grabbed her breasts.

"Ah shit Raelyn." she moaned.

"Mmmm." I moaned as I tasted her and felt Shawn pounding harder into me.

"Oooo right there." Paris moaned.

"Mmm. Fuck." Shawn moaned.

"Ahhhh I'm cuming." Paris said. She paused and tilted her head up to the ceiling, and then she said, "Oh my gawd Raelyn."

She climbed off me, and then Shawn leaned down and kissed her juices off my lips. He pounded a little longer, and then he lost himself and busted.

"Fuck." he groaned as he pulled out.

He stepped back and said, "Y'all something serious."

Paris and I started laughing, and then she kissed me.

"You've never been with two women before?" Paris asked.

"Nah man." Shawn said.

"Well I guess tonight is your lucky night." Paris said.

He chuckled and said, "I guess it is."

"I know that you're not done yet." Paris said.

"I'm not done unless y'all are."

"Nope we're not." I said.

All of us took turns going into the bathroom to clean up. Once we were all back in my bedroom, I crawled on top of Paris and started kissing her. I kissed her body down to her peach and began flicking my tongue on her pearl. He stood back and watched me pleasure her. Once he was aroused again, he stepped behind me and inserted his tool inside my wet center again, and just like that we had begun round two. Shawn gave it to me from behind as I feasted on Paris, and then he pounded into Paris as I rode her face, and then she rode his face while I rode his tool. After we got ours, he got his again, and then the three of us passed out in my bed.

Shawn got up early the next morning. It was just after four o'clock in the morning. He said that he had to go and run some errands with his mom and he would call me later. He kissed me and told me to tell Paris that he said bye. I walked him to the door, locked it after he walked out, and then I crawled back into the bed next to Paris and went back to sleep.

Chapter 25

Eazy

"You're looking good." I said to Aleyah.

"Thank you." she said with a smile. She sat back down in the booth.

We were at a smoothie restaurant. I had her meet there because I was heading there after the gym. She was already seated with a smoothie in hand. She had ordered one for me and it was on the table waiting for me to get there. I slid into the booth across from her and picked up my cup.

"Did you order the right one?" I asked.

"I ordered everything you put into the text message." she said with a giggle.

I laughed and said, "Aight."

I took a sip from the straw in my cup and then I asked, "So, what's been up since the whole fiasco?"

"A lot." Aleyah said. She took a sip from her smoothie and said, "First thing is, Lamar and I are legally separated."

I put my smoothie cup down on the table and asked, "What?"

"Yea." she said.

"Damn, I'm sorry." I said.

"No, you're not, but it's ok." she said, and then she laughed.

I laughed, and then I picked my cup back up to take a sip of my smoothie. After I swallowed my sip, I said, "You're partially right."

"Um hum. Well, I'm pregnant."

"Oh wow."

"I know."

"Congrats."

"Thank you."

"Whose is it? I mean no disrespect." I said.

"Nah, it's cool. It's Lamar's."

"You sure?"

"Shut up. Positively sure."

"I wouldn't be honest if I didn't say that I'm a little jealous." I said.

"I know." Aleyah said.

She made eye contact with me for a few seconds, and then she looked out of the window.

"So, what's going on with old boy?" I asked.

"Man. He's claiming not guilty. He's saying that I made the whole thing up because I was drunk, and I went with him willingly."

"Get the fuck out of here."

"For real. I'm so over it. I wish that they would just sentence him."

"Wow, that dude is crazy."

"Yup. he is."

"I just don't understand what happened." I said.

"I know. I didn't want to tell you because I was afraid of you judging me."

"Judging you? Woman please. Do I look like my parents? Better yet yours?"

She laughed and said. "You have a point."

"Aight, so try me. I want to know what happened. How did you end up fucking your husbands best-friend? Were you just on some savage shit, or was it just an emotional attachment? What was it?"

"Lamar and I were swingers. We swung with him once, and the affair started after." she said.

The information blew me away. My eyebrows went up, and then I said, "What? Wow."

"Yea."

I shook my head and said, "Damn you're a bigger freak than I thought you were."

She laughed and threw something at me. "Shut up." she said.

"I'm just saying. So y'all were actually fucking other couples?" I asked.

"Yes. Most of it was happening while we lived in Atlanta. We only swung with his best friend and his girl once when new moved back here. They were the only couple we did it with since we've been here."

"Damn. I've never done no shit like that, and I don't think I would ever want to. Watch another dude fuck my wife? Naaaah." I said, and then I took a sip from my smoothie.

"Yea it really wasn't Lamar's thing either. It was all my idea. I was bored and wanting to spice up my marriage. In the end, I wish that I could take it all back."

"If you were fucking with me, you would have never been bored."

"Eazy. Too soon."

I chuckled and said, "I'm just saying."

"Whatever."

"I'm saying. If you weren't happy, like I knew you weren't, why not just leave?"

"I was just trying to make things work. It's not easy to just leave when you have a kid together. You know that. Look at all the shit you and Karina have gone through."

"I see what you're saying, but at the end of the day, I don't feel like parents should stay together for the kids. Because I feel like kids know when their parents aren't happy. That's not a healthy environment to raise a kid in. I think that separating might be hard for them, but it is something that they will understand later in life. I feel like it would be harder for them to live in a household with two people that don't get along."

"Yea, but two parent households are better than one."

"Not in every case. If my parents didn't love each other the way they do, I would rather them be apart. I would've hated to have to hear them argue all the time like me and Karina. That's why I choose not to be with her. It's for the sake of our daughter, so she won't grow up crazy because of her parents."

"I understand." Aleyah said.

"Anyways, I'm glad that you're alright. Don't ever scare me like that again. Ok?"

"Ok."

"I love you woman."

"I love you too Eazy."

She took a sip from her smoothie, and then she asked, "So, what happened with you and that chick at the club?"

"Oh Tiffani? You know Karina sabotaged that."

She laughed, "New Year's Eve night?"

"Yup."

"Wow."

"I know. Karina won't let a brotha live."

"That's because she loves you."

"Yea, whatever. She loves herself."

"She loves herself too, but she loves you."

"Yea, but I can't deal with her on that level no more man. She's been asking me to get back together lately too, but I'm not with it. Plus, you know where my heart is. With a woman stuck in an unhealthy relationship that she's not happy in."

"Anyways. Also, because that woman's best-friend is in love with you."

"I'm not about to be arguing all the time about stupid shit."

"I hear you."

"Well since I can't have the love of my life, I'll settle when the right one comes along."

"Why do you have to settle? Why can't she be the one?"

"Because she's not you." I said.

She exhaled and looked me in my eyes. For a second, I wanted to reach over and kiss her, but I held back and respected her boundaries.

She said, "Honestly, and don't tell Karina I said this, but I thought the girl that you were with at the club with was really pretty, and you two looked good together."

I exhaled, "Yea, she was a good girl. I liked her more than I thought I was going to, but it's done now."

"Have you ever thought about just apologizing to her? A good apology can solve most things."

"Yea, but I don't know if it's even worth it."

"Ok, well, I got to go." she said as she stood up.

"Aight. Well, hit me up, and let me know what happens with that fuck boy."

"I will."

Chapter 26

Riley

Mike was walking around the house bouncing Riley's daughter in his arms and patting her on the back. He walked from one end of the room to the other a few times. He looked down at her to see if she had settled down. She had been a little fussy and Riley was at her wits end, so Mike stepped in to see if he could help. Raina had stopped crying and looked like she was falling asleep, so he continued to bounce her and walk around the house.

"You know you look good with a baby in your arms." Riley said.

"Man stop." Mike replied.

Riley laughed and said, "Seriously. Have you ever thought about being a daddy?"

"Once or twice, but I don't have time for this." Mike said.

"Why not?" Riley asked.

"It's too much work."

"Yea, but you do it so naturally."

"I guess." he said as he handed the sleeping baby to Riley.

Riley stood up with the baby in her arms, walked the baby to her basinet, and laid her in it. She gently slid the blanket over her baby, and then she turned on the baby monitor. She tip-toed back over to the couch and sat down next to Mike.

"Congratulations on your new book." Riley said after she sat down.

"Thanks." Mike said.

"You're welcome. How does it feel being at number one?"

"It feels good. I'm proud of myself."

"You should be. I'm proud of you too."

"Thank you, so what are we watching tonight?"

"It's Wednesday, so you know what that means. Empire and Star."

"Aight cool. I can watch those, and then I've got to go. My friend is coming through."

"Same girl as the last time?"

"Yes."

Riley said, "Ok."

"What? Don't make that face. We are just working on a project."

"Ok."

Riley laid her head on his shoulder and turned the television sound up a little. She was slightly irritated, but she didn't say anything. That was the third time that week that his *friend* had visited to work on a project. That wasn't even counting all the other times she had been over to Mike's house since Riley had the baby. In Riley's opinion, the chick was hanging around too much to be just a *friend*. On top of that, he had went out to breakfast with another one of his friends to celebrate his book release the day before.

"You better stop with that attitude." Mike said.

"I don't have one."

"Yes, you do, but it's cute though. Give me those angry lips." he said, and then he leaned down to kiss her.

"Stop." she said.

"Don't tell me to stop. I'm not stopping until you stop being mad." Mike said.

He continued to kiss her until she started laughing.

"Okaayyy." Riley sang.

"That's right." he said, and then he kissed her again. The kiss turned serious and more passionate than the first few. They kissed for a while.

"Damn, I love kissing you." Mike said.

"I love kissing you too." Riley said.

Mike kissed Riley more, and then he reached down and touched her breasts. Riley reached over and touched the crotch of his jeans.

He stopped kissing her, and said, "Don't start shit that you're not ready for."

"I'm ready."

"You just had a baby Ri."

"So."

"So, you need time to heal."

"I went to the doctor. I've been healed for a while."

"Emotionally too?"

"Yea." Riley said.

Mike said, "Anyways. We're missing the show."

"I'm serious."

"Um hum. That's what you say. I'm not about to get caught up in no Love Triangle messing with you. I ain't got time."

"Love Triangle?"

"Yea."

She laughed and said, "Ah ok. Mr. We are Working on a Project."

Mike started laughing and said, "You're a trip. Do you know that? Ms. I Love My Baby Daddy. I'll never let him go."

Riley laughed again. "Wow you're wrong for that." she said.

"I'm just saying."

"Whatever. You don't see him around, do you?"

"No."

"Well, then."

"Let's watch this show." Mike said.

He kissed her again, and then they turned their attention to the television and begin watching the show.

***

Riley was relieved that the winter season was close to being over. She'd had enough of the snow and ice and having the baby made it more difficult to get around. She never imagined there would be so much to do to leave the house just to do something simple like go to the store. She had to get herself dressed, get the baby dressed, run downstairs to start the car, run back upstairs to pack a diaper bag, get the baby bundled up, get herself bundled up, and then carry the baby, the diaper bag, and her purse down the stairs. Walk carefully over snow and ice to the car, strap the baby in, brush snow off the car, and then get into the car to go. That day, the sun was out, and the snow was almost melted away. That eliminated two steps from her routine, and she didn't have to worry about possibly falling on ice while carrying the baby. She prayed that it wasn't going to snow again, but she knew that the weather was unpredictable. Snow could fall in May in Minnesota. It wasn't even March yet.

Riley looked back at the baby to make sure that she was alright and had her pacifier in her mouth before pulling off. She was on her way to the store to pick up some food for Cherry's visit. She didn't feel like cooking, but she didn't have much in her house to snack on, and she hated having people over and not having anything to feed them with. She pulled up to the store a few minutes later. After getting her daughter out of the backseat, she walked over to get a cart. She put the baby in the cart and headed into the store. Once in the store, she heard her video chat notification ringing. She knew that it was Jamir calling to check on the baby. She pulled out her phone and swiped the screen to answer it.

"Hey Ri." he said when he saw her face on the screen.

"Hey."

"What you doing?"

"I'm at the grocery store picking up some things."

"Where's Raina?"

"She's right here."

"Let me see her."

Riley pushed the button that flips the camera from her to the rear camera, so he could see the baby.

"Look at my pretty baby. She's getting so big." Jamir said.

"I know." Riley said, and then she turned the camera back to her.

"I'm gonna come and see her soon. I want to come to your crib though. I don't want to go to your parent's house. They be looking at me crazy."

"I don't know about coming to my house."

"Come on Ri. I'm just coming through to see my baby. That's it."

"I don't know Jamir."

"It shouldn't be that hard. Why are you acting funny?"

"Because we've had so much drama at my house. I'm not trying have all that going on again."

"You're not. I'm just coming to see my daughter and that's it."

"I'll think about it." Riley said.

"Anyways. My mom wants to see the baby. She told me to ask you to see if you will bring the baby by her house."

"You told her?"

"Yea I did. I felt like she should know that she has another grandchild in the world. She wants to meet you and get to know you and her new grandchild, so think about that too."

"I will, but I have to go. I need to pay for my things."

"Give my daughter a kiss for me."

"I will." Riley said.

She disconnected the all, put the phone back into her purse, and began scanning her items at the self-check-out register. Riley paid for her things and headed back to her house. She made it back right on time because Cherry was pulling up. Cherry parked her car behind Riley's and got out.

"Let me help you with those bags. You can get Raina."

"Thank you, girl." Riley said as she handed the bags to Cherry.

Riley grabbed the baby's car seat, diaper bag, and her purse and followed Cherry to the door.

"I'm so glad that this snow is almost gone." Cherry said as they walked up the stairs to Riley's apartment.

"Me too girl. I can't wait for Spring."

"If we have one girl. You know how this weather is." Cherry said, and then she put the bags on Riley's kitchen counter.

"I know." Riley said.

She set the car seat on the couch, unstrapped the baby, and pulled her out.

"Oh my gosh. Look how big she's gotten." Cherry said.

"I know. She eats a lot."

"Aww let me hold my fat baby." Cherry said.

She walked over and took the baby from Riley's arms. Riley headed into the kitchen to put the groceries away.

"I didn't feel like cooking, so I got us some pizza's, chips, and soda. Is that cool?"

"Girl, is that cool for you? You know you and your sister are the health nuts."

"I know. I've been off diet since I've had this baby. I need to get back on track, but she's been wearing me out."

"Don't you go back to work soon?"

"Yes, and school. I don't know how I'm going to do it."

"Girl women do it all the time. You got this."

"Thank you. I am going to enjoy this last little bit of time off that I have left."

"You better." Cherry laughed.

"Who's going to watch her while you are work?"

"Girl I was going to send her to daycare, but it's way too expensive, so my little cousin is going to watch her. She just graduated high school and she isn't working, so she said she wanted to make some money. She is a good girl, so I know Raina will be in good hands."

"Oh, that's cool."

"Yea, it's much cheaper. She took a couple of years off from school, so I'll just have to figure something out when she starts college."

Riley put the frozen pizzas into the oven and walked back into the living room. She sat on the couch next to Cherry.

"Girl, she looks just like you and your sister."

"You think so? I think she looks like her dad. I'm not surprised either as much as I hated him when I was pregnant with her."

Cherry laughed. "My mama believes that myth whole heartedly. She would always tell my aunts don't hate anyone while you're pregnant or your baby will come out looking like them."

Riley laughed. "My mom used to say the same thing."

"So, what's been up with Jamir anyways?"

"I just talked to him while I was at the store. He was calling to check on Raina. He wants to come over here and see her."

"Are you going to let him?"

"I don't know yet. I really don't want to. Especially with all the drama that happened over here, and with Mike downstairs. It would feel kind of awkward."

"Yea, but you and Mike aren't together, right?"

"No, we're not."

"I mean, are you fucking him?"

"No."

"It shouldn't be awkward then."

"Yea. You have a point."

"What's going on with y'all anyways?"

"I don't know girl. We're just chilling."

"Y'all ain't talking about being more than just friends. You two make a really cute couple."

"Thanks, but we haven't really talked about it. He thinks that I'm still trying to get over Jamir."

"Are you over Jamir?"

"I think that I am."

"Have you told him that?"

"Yea."

"Maybe he's just trying to take his time with you."

"I don't know girl because Mike hasn't had a girlfriend for a long time, and I'm not sure that is something that he really wants. He might be content with having me as his friend with the possibility of maybe having some casual sex here and there."

"Like a friend with benefits situation?"

"Yea, and the thing is, he has a lot of female friends."

"Like a lot of female friends with benefits?"

"That, I don't know. He claims he's not fucking any of them, but he is always with one of them."

"Where is he at now?"

"Out having lunch with one of his female friends."

"Oh wow."

"I know, and that's not it. Last week he went to breakfast with one, and the week before that, one of them had stopped over his house a few times to help him with some project."

"What kind of project?"

"He said that he is working on putting a podcast together."

"You sure it's not a come and help me bust a nut project?"

Riley laughed. "Right. I don't know. I like Mike, and I don't think that he would lie to me, but I'm not going to get myself caught up in another situation with a dude that has secrets and side chicks."

"I feel you on that girl."

"Yea, so I don't know.

The baby started whining a little, so Riley asked Cherry to continue holding her while she made her a bottle and took the pizzas out of the oven. Riley headed to the kitchen. She looked out the window and saw Mike pulling up in front of the house. She watched him get out of the car and walk to the house, and then she finished what she was doing.

***

After Cherry left, she got her baby to sleep, she checked her phone to check her text messages. Mike had texted her to see if she was still up and if her company had left. She didn't respond. She texted Jamir and told him that the baby was fine and was asleep. She heard a few knocks at the door below. She knew that it was Mike because he didn't want to ring the doorbell, so he wouldn't wake the baby up. She walked quietly down the stairs to answer the door.

When she opened it, he said, "Hey."

"Hey. What you doing here?"

"What do you mean? I come over here every night."

"I'm surprised that you're not with one of your friends."

"Riley."

"I'm just saying."

"I take it, you're mad at me?"

"Nope."

"Can I come in?"

"Yep."

Riley opened the door to let him in. He closed it quietly, locked it, and followed her up the stairs.

"Is the baby sleep?"

"Yep."

"I figured that. That is why I knocked. Look, why are you tripping?"

"I'm not."

"Yes, you are. Just like you were before."

"I'm not. You just seem to have a lot of friends."

"I do. I told you that though."

"I guess I didn't expect it to be so many."

"So many?" Mike chuckled.

"Yea."

"They are just women that I went to school with and women that I used to work with, but it's not anything more than just business."

"You're trying to tell me not one of those women are trying to get with you, or don't be flirting with you?"

"Most of the time they don't. If they do, I know how to skate around that."

"I guess. I'm not tripping anyways. I guess I kind of liked the idea of me being your only friend."

"You're my only friend that I see and think about every day. You're my only special friend. We basically spend the night with each other every night. I'm not doing that with anyone else."

"Don't you think that's because I live here, so it's almost like we live together?" Riley asked.

"I see what you're saying." Mike chuckled, and then he reached for her. He pulled her to him and said, "Come here. Get that frown off your face."

"Whatever." Riley said.

"Nah, but for real. I'm trying to get this podcast together. I've been trying to pick a couple of co-hosts and someone who can film it for social media. I want women because I feel that women can touch on topics that I might not think of as a man. I also want a woman's perspective on the show. I don't want it to be bias, masculine, and just about what I think. So, I've been reaching out to a lot of people that I know, but trust me, it's just business. You have nothing to worry about. You're still the number one woman in my life."

"Yea but I'm not your woman, and I've been down this road before, so it is what it is."

"What does that mean?"

"It doesn't mean nothing. It means we're friends, and you don't owe me an explanation."

"Riley."

"What? Are you hungry?" Because I'm hungry." she chuckled.

Mike stared at her for a second, and then he chuckled. "Yea I am actually. I've been working all day."

"You wanna order something?"

"That's cool."

"You want to order take out, or delivery?"

"It doesn't matter. If we choose take-out, I can go and pick it up."

"Ok. Take-out it is. I have menus on the fridge."

Chapter 27

Shawn

The threesome with Raelyn and her friend Paris caught me by surprise. I wasn't expecting that at all from Raelyn. I'm a man so of course I was excited about having my first experience with two women, but part of me wasn't sure how to feel about it. Up until that night, I didn't even know Raelyn went that way. I wasn't aware of her and Paris's history at all, so the entire experience had my mind blown. I couldn't stop thinking about it. Every time I was focusing on something else an image of them kissing would pop up in my mind.

"Shawn." my mom called my name.

"Huh?" I replied. Hearing her call my name broke me from my thoughts about Raelyn and Paris.

"You didn't hear me calling you?" she asked.

"No mom. I'm sorry."

"Where was your mind at?" she asked.

"A bunch of different places mom. I'm sorry."

"It's ok. You were probably thinking about that girl. Hand me that smaller paint brush so I can get the top of this wall."

I picked up the brush, dipped it in the tan colored paint, and handed it to my mom. I was helping her paint her bedroom a different color, and then she wanted me to come back over the next weekend to help her repaint the living room. She'd just bought new furniture for her house and she wanted the room colors to match her new décor.

"Why are you painting this room tan anyways."

"It matches my new bed set and wall art."

"Why didn't you pick something simple like a white and black theme."

"Boy this is simple. I just wanted neutral colors like tan, brown, and gold."

"I can't wait to see this when it's all done."

"Me too. Anyways. How is she doing anyways?"

"Who?"

"The pretty girl that you introduced me to. What was her name Roslyn?"

"Oh. You mean Raelyn mom."

"Yes. Raelyn. How is she? You know that I really like her. When are y'all going to become an item?"

A thought about Raelyn, Paris, and myself sexing each other crazy crossed my mind, and then I said, "She is fine. I know that you like her, but I don't think that she is interested in me like that mom. I don't think she wants to be more than just friends."

"Give it some time. She'll come around. Sometimes it takes us women a little longer to see what's good for us."

I sucked my teeth and said, "You're just saying that because I'm your son."

"Yes. I am saying that because you're my son, but I'm also saying it because you're a good guy. You deserve a good woman, and I think she is it. She just doesn't know it yet."

"Ok mom. Well, I wouldn't have my eyes set on her just yet."

"Just take your time son, and if it doesn't work it just doesn't. I guess that means that the right one will come along at some point. As long as she is nothing like your last girl. That witch."

I chuckled, "Mom don't start."

"I'm sorry, but you know I can't stand her."

"I know."

"She wasn't no good for nobody. She wasn't any good for herself. You know I saw her at the mall one day looking all tore up from the floor up. Had some long blonde weave all down her back and some booty shorts all up the crack of her behind. She was pushing her baby in a stroller and had the nerve to smile and speak to me. I barely spoke back."

"I know mom. You told me."

"She was always in the streets, always drinking, always clubbing. I wonder who that baby is by. I'm sure it ain't the dude she cheated on you with. She probably doesn't even know who the child's father is."

I started laughing. "Ok mom. Stop. Leave that girl alone. I'm not with her no more." I said through laughs.

"I'm glad, and I'm glad that you didn't have any babies with her. Thank God."

"I know. I say the same thing mom." I said.

"Yea well anyways."

She got down from the ladder, and then both of us stepped back to look at our work.

My mom nodded her head and said, "It looks really good. Exactly how I wanted it. I can't wait to get my furniture in here."

"When is it coming?"

"Monday."

"Ok. Well, are you hungry? Because I am."

"Yea I am."

"Well let's go get something to eat, my treat."

"That's what I like to hear. My son treating me out to eat." she smiled.

"You're so silly mom. You can pick the place."

"Alright, well let me get cleaned up quick, and then we can go."

"Ok. I'm gonna go wash my hands and face in the guest bathroom."

***

I had talked to Raelyn through text, but I hadn't seen Raelyn since the night we had the threesome. She said that she was having some friends and family over to play cards and have drinks, so she invited me. It was close to the Easter holiday which meant her birthday was coming up. I wanted to plan something special for her to show her how much I love her, so I figured it would be the perfect time to pick her friends and families brains to get some ideas. When I walked into her place, a few people were already there. Her friends Taji and Cherry were sitting on the couch, and her God-sister Aleyah was sitting in a chair.

"Hey!" Raelyn said when she saw me.

She was walking out of the kitchen with a glass of wine in hand. She walked up to me and hugged me, and then she told me that we were waiting for a few more people and to make myself comfortable. She handed the glass she had in her hands to Cherry, and then she asked me if I wanted something. I told her what I wanted to drink, and then she walked back to the kitchen.

"Where's Paris and Riley?" Cherry asked.

"They'll be here in a minute. Riley had to drop Raina off at our parent's house and Paris had something to do, but they both text me and said that they would be here." Raelyn said.

"Oh ok." Cherry said.

"Taji are you drinking tonight?" Raelyn asked.

"No. I'm still breastfeeding."

"Ok. When are you bringing your son by to spend time with his Auntie Rae? I haven't seen him since you had him."

"I know. Girl he keeps me busy. I can't believe I'm out right now. His dad was brave enough to keep him."

"You have a good man girl." Raelyn said.

"Thanks." Taji said.

"You're welcome. I can always stop by and see him. Just let me know when you're free." Raelyn said as she walked out of the kitchen with my drink in hand.

Raelyn handed me the drink, and then Riley walked in.

"Yo!" Riley said.

She walked around the room and hugged everyone including me, and then she sat down on the other side of the sectional couch. Raelyn walked back into the kitchen to make a drink for Riley.

"So how did things turn out with that situation?" Taji asked Aleyah.

"Well I can confirm that it was just a rumor, so me and hubby are straight." Aleyah said.

"That's good." Cherry said.

"Thank God." Aleyah said.

I knew that they were talking about something that I didn't know about, so I just listened. I've learned from my mom and my aunties to just stay quiet and listen when women get to chatting. They will forget that you are there and spill it all.

"Yes. For real. Me and hubby are still separated, but counseling has been helping and we've been getting our thing back together."

"That's good."

"What about Niko?"

"Girl they finally sentenced him. He got fifteen years in prison, so we won't be seeing him for a while."

"Too bad they didn't lock his ass up for good." Riley said.

"I know, but I'm glad they gave him some time. Now, my husband and I can work on fixing our marriage and focus on this pregnancy."

"I hear that. I'm praying for you two, even though you know who we wish you were with." Raelyn said.

"Girl don't start." Aleyah said.

Riley and Raelyn started laughing, and then Paris showed up. Raelyn and Riley's brother showed up with a couple of his friends after Paris. I put my phone down and slapped hands with the fellas. I was kind of glad to see the fellas there because I was starting to feel out-numbered. Riley's guy friend Mike was the last one to show up, and then Raelyn put some music on, set up the card tables, and we got a couple of card games going.

Towards the end of the night Raelyn and I whooped a few people, and then everyone took another break to refill drinks and use the bathroom. I had already talked to Aleyah, Taji, and Cherry. While Raelyn was in the bathroom, I approached Paris.

"How have you been?" I asked.

She smiled and said, "I've been good. How have you been?"

"I've been well." I responded. I was glad that there wasn't any awkward energy between us. We hadn't seen each other since the threesome.

"You know our girl bday is coming up." I said.

"I know." she said.

I want to do something special for her. Like a surprise, but I need help planning it. You are the closest one to her right now, so I would like to run some ideas by you."

"Oh my gosh. That would be so dope. She would so love you for that Shawn."

"That's what I'm hoping, so are you down to help me plan it?"

"Hell yea. Here let me put my number in your phone, and then we can get together to brainstorm. Oh my gosh she is going to love it. I'm too excited." Paris said as she put her number in my phone.

She gave me my phone back and asked if I wanted a refill of my drink. I told her that I did, and then Raelyn returned from the bathroom.

"Who's next to get that ass spanked?" Raelyn asked.

"I'm on Raelyn's table." Eazy said.

"Me too." Aleyah said.

"Aight you my partner." Eazy said.

"You ready to get this whipping girl?" Eazy asked Raelyn.

"Shut up brother. You ain't talking about nothing." Raelyn said. She walked past him and popped him upside his head before sitting down.

"Sup bro you ready?" he asked me.

"Yup." I said.

I slapped hands with him to show him respect, and then we started the game. Raelyn and I whooped them, so they asked for a rematch, and then we whooped them again. They left our table, we played against a few more people, and then everyone left to go home.

Chapter 28

Riley

Riley put the baby in her crib, and then quietly walked out of the room and shut the door behind her.

"Are you thirsty?" Riley asked Jamir.

"Yea, what you got?"

"Water and juice." she said as she headed into the kitchen.

Jamir stood up and followed her into the kitchen. "I'll take water." he said.

"Is Aquafina ok?" she asked.

"Yup. That's cool." he said.

Riley opened the refrigerator and pulled a bottle of water out for herself and one out for Jamir. She closed the refrigerator and handed one of the bottles of water to him, and then she opened her bottle of water. She took a few gulps from the bottle, and then she put the cap back on it.

"Thanks for letting me come through and see my daughter."

"You're welcome."

Riley thought about when he made the decision to let Jamir stop by her house to see their daughter. Mike was on one of his business lunches with one of his female friends again. When Jamir called, she told him that he could stop by for a visit. She felt awkward the entire time he was there.

"To be honest, I was kind of getting tired of being at my parents' house anyways. I can't believe she fell asleep in your arms like that. She never falls asleep for me. Only when I feed her; other than that, she is up."

"That's cause that's daddy's baby."

"Whatever. She is going to be a mama's girl."

"Nah man. That's daddy's little girl."

"Yea ok." Riley laughed.

"I miss you." Jamir said.

Riley rolled her eyes.

"I do." Jamir said.

He stepped to her, pulled her chin to him, and then he kissed her. She kissed him back, and then he pushed her body up against the refrigerator. Riley felt some of her old feelings return, and then she felt his hand on her butt. Riley was turned on, but she stopped kissing him.

"Stop Jamir." she said.

"What?" he asked.

"We're not supposed to be doing this."

"You're right. I'm sorry. I'm tripping."

"It's ok."

"You don't miss me?"

Riley sighed. "I'm not answering that question."

"Why? Because you do?"

"The fact of the matter is, you're still married, and I'm not going through that again."

"You're right, but that doesn't change how I feel about you."

"Well it changed how I felt about you."

"Damn, ok."

"Um, I think it's time for you to go now."

"You're kicking me out?"

"No. I'm asking you to leave. Raina is asleep, so the visit is over."

He chuckled, "Aight man. Can you at least bring our baby by my mom's house? She really wants to see her."

"So, I can run into Kiesha? Hell no. As a matter of fact, get up out of here before she realizes that you're over here." Riley said.

Jamir laughed and said, "Kiesha is never at my mom's because my mom can't stand her, so could you please bring her by, so my mom could quit asking me because I don't know what else to tell her. Please?"

Riley sighed and said, "Ok."

"Cool. I'll set it up."

The doorbell rang and caught their attention.

"Shit." Riley said as she turned to look out of the kitchen window.

She already knew who it was, but she was checking to make sure that it wasn't Keisha showing up to claim her husband again. She could see Mike standing on the porch, and she figured he probably saw Jamir's car parked out front.

"I'll be right back." she said to Jamir.

She hurried out of the door and down the stairs. Riley opened the door, but she stood in the doorway blocking Mike from walking in.

"Hey." she said.

"Hey." he replied. Her suspicious behavior caught him off guard.

"I thought that you would still be at your meeting."

"It ended early. What's up with you?"

"Oh nothing. I just put Raina to bed."

Riley cursed to herself when she heard Jamir's footsteps walking down the stairs behind her. She turned to see if it was Jamir, and then she turned back to look at Mike after she confirmed that it was Jamir.

Jamir said. "Aight Riley. I'll holla at you."

He opened the door to walk out. Mike and Jamir made eye contact with each other.

"Sup bruh?" Jamir said.

"Sup." Mike said.

Mike stepped back to let Jamir walk out of the door, and then he looked back at Riley. Riley looked down at the ground.

"I'll talk to you later." Mike said.

He turned and walked into his apartment. He slammed the door after walking in. Riley knew that Mike was angry, but she couldn't address it because Raina started crying. She closed her door and ran back up the stairs to tend to her daughter.

Chapter 29

Riley

Riley had just returned home from dropping Raina off with her mom. She was getting a much-needed break from her daily routine, and she had plans to spend her free time with Mike. She knew that Mike was probably still mad at her about the situation earlier that day, so she was hoping to at least get a chance to talk to him even if they didn't hang out. Riley had sent him a couple of text messaged while she was at her parent's house that he didn't respond to right away, but he finally told her that they could still hang out.

Riley rang Mike's doorbell when she made it back home. He didn't answer after the first ring, so she rang it again.

"It's open!" he called out.

Riley walked in and closed the door. She headed into the kitchen where Mike was. He was preparing some food. He didn't take his eyes off the stove to acknowledge her.

"Hey." she said.

"What's up?" he asked.

He turned the stove off, put the lid over the pot, and then he put the spoon on the stove.

"Are you mad at me?"

"Nah." Mike said.

He turned towards the sink to rinse off a few plates, and then he turned to put them on the counter; all without looking at Riley.

"Mike talk to me." she said.

"About what?" he asked.

"About earlier." she said.

Riley walked over to him and stood in front of him and asked, "Can you look at me?"

Mike stopped what he was doing and gave Riley the eye contact that she was asking for.

"So, you had your baby daddy over because of me having lunch with my homegirls?"

"No."

"That's what it looks like to me." he said angrily.

"It wasn't like that."

"So, what was it like?"

"He called and asked if he could stop by to visit her, so I told him that he could."

"Because I was at lunch with one of my homegirls."

"No."

"Yea alright, well, that's your business. If that's what you want, then go ahead."

Mike turned back to the stove, opened the oven, used an oven mitten to pull out a pan of food. He put the pan on top of the stove, put the oven mitten on the counter, and then he turned the stove off.

"Mike." Riley said, but he ignored her.

She repeated his name again, and then he said, "Riley I ain't with the bullshit."

"Mike. I don't want him. I want you."

"That's what you say."

"That's what I mean."

"Are you sure?"

"Yes."

Mike shook his head, and then he said, "I know that we've been dancing around this, and I want you too Riley, but I can't with the drama."

"I'm not with all these female friends, and this no titles mess. I did that with him. I'm not doing it again. I need to know that I'm yours and your mine, and I need everyone else to know that too."

Mike shook his head again, exhaled loudly, and then he said, "It's been a long time since I've been in a relationship, but I'm doing this because I'm in love with you. Just to let you know, all my female friends know how I feel about you, so if I go into this and put us out there, I need to know that you are serious."

"I'm in love with you too, and I am serious, so what are you saying?"

"I'm asking are we going to make this official and be together?"

"Really?"

"Really."

Riley smiled. "Yes, we can make this official."

"Alright then, don't be on no bullshit Riley."

"I'm not."

"Ok."

"So, does this mean that I'm your bae now?"

"You've been my bae."

Riley smiled as Mike leaned down to kiss Riley. She wrapped her hands around his neck while returning the feverish kiss. He picked her up and put her on the counter. Mike pulled her panties off and pushed her dress up above her waist. Riley unbuttoned his jeans, and then Mike pulled his manhood out. He put it inside her and Riley closed her eyes and got lost in the feeling of him inside of her. It had been a while since she had felt a man grace the walls of her flower. She wrapped her hands around his back and pulled him close to her as she grinded into him. He used the counter to keep his balance while he thrusted into her. They kissed, and then he sucked on her neck while she moaned his name and whispered that she loved him.

"I love you too." Mike whispered.

He picked her up off the counter. Riley wrapped her legs around him, and then she bounced on him while they kissed. They stood there making love in the middle of the kitchen with all the lights on for a while. He put her back on the counter, and then he told her to hold onto the counter. She unwrapped her legs, slid off the counter, turned around and grabbed the counter. Mike entered her from the back.

"Ooooh Mike." Riley moaned.

"It feels good?" Mike asked.

"Yeess." she said.

"You feel good." he said.

He did a combination of thrusting, pounding, and grinding into her. She bounced back which made him go even harder. He grabbed her waist and pulled her to him.

She moaned louder and continued to bounce on his manhood until she got hers, and then he got his. Mike pulled out and caught his seeds in his hand.

"Damn girl you got some good pussy."

Riley laughed, "Ewww. I've never heard you talk like that."

Mike laughed, "I'm just stating facts."

"Well, you got some good dick."

"You liked that?"

"Yea." Riley smiled.

"You want some more?"

"Yea."

Mike kissed her and said, "Come on let's go in my room."

Mike made sure the stove and oven were off. He turned off the kitchen light, and then Riley followed him into his bedroom. The spent the entire night making love to each other, and then Riley got up the next morning and made them breakfast. She was excited. She finally had a man that was all hers.

Continue to Finale….

Contact

niarichbooks@gmail.com

Nia Rich